THE AUTHOR

Clifford Henry Benn Kitchin was born in Harrogate, Yorkshire, in 1895. He was educated at Clifton College, Bristol, from where he won a classical scholarship to Exeter College, Oxford. From 1916-18 he served in the British Army in France, and after the war turned to the Law, joining Lincoln's Inn and being called to the Bar in 1924. Later, like the hero of his crime novels, Malcolm Warren, he became a stockbroker, but a huge inherited fortune allowed him to leave his profession and to concentrate on his great love, writing.

His first two novels, *Streamers Waving* and *Mr Balcony*, were published by Leonard and Virginia Woolf at The Hogarth Press in 1924 and 1925. He won wide popularity with his detective novels, *Death of My Aunt* (1929), *Crime at Christmas* (1934) and *Death of His Uncle* (1939), all published as Hogarth paperbacks, interspersed with more serious novels, the most famous of which is *The Auction Sale* (1949).

The unique atmosphere of Kitchin's detective fiction owes a lot to his own eccentricity. Scholarly, humorous, given to sudden caprices, he was an expert botanist, poet, linguist, fine chess player and talented musician, with the unnerving habit of composing improvisations to illustrate his friends' characters. An avid collector of priceless objects, whether Georgian silver or Meissen teapots, he was also well-known as a gambler on London greyhound tracks and in Riviera casinos. In the end, however, despite his daunting, rapier wit, his death in 1967 drew tributes to, above all, his sensitivity and generosity of spirit.

MR BALCONY
C.H.B. Kitchin

"Ce phénomène, beaucoup de gens superficiels
le traduisent par le mot égoïsme."

— BALZAC

New Introduction by Francis King

THE HOGARTH PRESS
LONDON

To Richard Jennings

Published in 1989 by
The Hogarth Press
30 Bedford Square
London WC1B 3SG

Originally published in Great Britain by The Hogarth Press 1927

A CIP catalogue record for this book is available from the British Library.

ISBN 0 7012 0630 6

Printed in Great Britain by
Cox & Wyman Ltd
Reading, Berkshire

INTRODUCTION

Mr Balcony is both the strangest of Clifford Kitchin's novels and one of the strangest to appear in the twenties. One senses that, at a period when there were still areas of life into which a novelist entered at his peril, the author was constantly engaged in slipping things past his publishers, past his public, and even perhaps – like L.P. Hartley, so strangely unaware of some of the implications of his books – past his own self. Just as the precise nature of the Heart of Darkness that engulfs Conrad's Kurtz is left, through a series of ominously teasing hints, for the reader to infer, so too is the precise nature of the Heart of Darkness into which Mr Balcony voluntarily precipitates himself as an act of self-immolation.

A further reason for the book's strangeness is the contrast between the playful iridescence of its surface and the murky sombreness of its theme. Dazzled by that iridescence, the eye of the reader may be rendered incapable of glimpsing the monsters churning far below in its depths.

The key to Kitchin's intentions seems to me to lie in an extract from that pile of manuscripts, tied up with red tape, that Mr Balcony, their author, takes from a locked drawer in his house off Brompton Road (Kitchin himself for a long time had a house off Brompton Road, in Montpelier Square) and begins to read over. "...It was on that day that I first conceived the idea of altering my character, of doing violence to myself, and being all that nature had not intended me to be, and nothing that she had." It is this idea – indeed, obsession – that impels Mr Balcony to use what remains of an inherited fortune to hire a luxury yacht to take him and a strange assortment of acquaintances to a primitive African country and finally to submit to a fate that, because of the prohibitions in force at that period, is described so allusively that Jan Morris's title for a book later narrating a not dissimilar experience, *Conundrum*, might have stood as

Kitchin's heading to this vital chapter.

Mr Balcony reminds one of his neighbours, later to be among those who accompany him to Africa, "of the late Lord Kitchener when younger". Kitchener was, of course, a man of whom it might be said that he had "done violence to his natural character", thus becoming "all that nature had not intended me to be". But Mr Balcony is not merely, in some respects, like Kitchener. He is also, in many respects, like Kitchin. Like Kitchin he has inherited money, which he has multiplied by a combination of shrewdness and daring on the Stock Exchange. Like Kitchin, too, he is one of those men who, in more innocent times, were described as "confirmed bachelors" or "not the marrying kind". So it comes about that, after the arrival of the weirdly heterogeneous party of travellers in Africa, Mr Balcony recklessly sets out to "do himself a last piece of violence, to make himself different from what nature had intended him to be, a bachelor".

In the last and least successful of his novels, *A Short Walk in Williams Park*, Kitchin would again have as his central character a man who uses his wealth to dominate and direct, albeit far more gently, other people's lives. This was an occupation in which Kitchin himself delighted. To many he was extremely generous with his money, but that money had to be used as he, not they, willed. Thus, when I had retired prematurely from the British Council in order to devote myself exclusively to writing, he decided that I must have a house and that he would supplement my meagre savings to enable me to buy one. But, since he himself was then spending more and more of his time in Brighton, it was in Brighton that the house must be located; and since he had decided, I do not know why, that the only style for me was Regency, it was a Regency house that, with his assistance, I eventually acquired.

Again like his Mr Balcony, Kitchin seemed constantly to be striving to bend the twig of his character in a direction opposite to that in which it would naturally have grown. One would hardly have expected such a man enthusiastically to take up photography, acquiring a Leica and Bronica and even developing and enlarging his work in a darkroom of his own; to parade with his greyhounds at White City; or to study algebra and mathematics while confined to bed during his last illness. Even his final choice of a sexual partner suggested the action of a man determined to do precisely the opposite of what everyone expected of him. When I first came to know him, he would constantly refer to "my friend George" – telling me that he could not have dinner with me on Tuesday because that was the evening when George would be visiting him, or saying of some story of mine: "Oh, I must tell George that. That'll tickle him." Since I was never allowed to meet George, since Kitchin never told me anything about him, and since he was not the kind of man I felt that I could interrogate until I came to know him far better, I used to try to imagine what George would be like. Yes, he would be a rough, North Country guardsman, of the kind that appealed to my friend Joe Ackerley. Or perhaps a policeman, like E.M. Forster's chum? One day, without warning, I rang the bell of the Montpelier Square house, in order to leave off a book that I had promised to lend to Kitchin. The door was opened by an elderly, working-class man in slippers, whom I immediately assumed to be standing in for Kitchin's manservant Sidney. I asked for "Mr Kitchin" and the dear old buffer then preceded me up the stairs to the first-floor sitting-room, panting heavily. When Kitchin greeted me, he said, more gleeful than embarrassed: "Francis, I don't believe you've met George." George, now dead, was married and even older than Kitchin.

As in the case of Mr Balcony, one often wondered to what extent Kitchin's godlike interventions in other people's lives – he frequently intervened in those of George and his family – were motivated by affection and to what extent by curiosity and the satisfaction that the exercise of power so often brings with it. The manner in which he "collected" the most unlikely people, his lifelong friend L.P. Hartley once suggested to me, was not dissimilar to the manner in which he collected *objets de vertu*. It was Hartley's contention that Kitchin did not buy pictures, pieces of Georgian silver or antique paperweights out of affection for these things but because he derived supreme pleasure from first their acquisition and then their possession.

When he eventually decided to dispose of this or that piece, he did so without a qualm. Hartley concluded (I remember his words as best I can): "Whether he is collecting objects or people, I always feel that Clifford tends to display more knowledge than taste." Their relationship was one strangely compounded of affection and rancour.

When I once told Hartley that, of Kitchin's books, *Mr Balcony* was the one that, for all its ambiguities, I liked the best, he surprised me by remarking: "Of course, you realise that Mr Balcony is meant to be me." The thought had never for a moment occurred to me; indeed I am still, after all these years, surprised and bewildered by the claim. In his introduction to *A Short Walk in Williams Park*, Hartley put forward the theory that the reason why, despite the enthusiasm of reviewers, popular success had always eluded his friend, was that that hypercritical intelligence made readers feel that he was "getting at" them. Perhaps, when he had read *Mr Balcony* as a young man, Hartley had had the same suspicion. After all, until old age and a change in popular attitudes had loosened him up, Hartley had spent his life "doing violence", like Mr Balcony, to his true nature.

Certainly, the relationship between Kitchin and Hartley was ambivalent in the warring emotions of which it was compounded. Kitchin, whose *The Book of Life* is both similar in theme to Hartley's *The Go-Between* and in no way its inferior, could not understand why it had not enjoyed a comparable success. Hartley, in turn, had the uneasy suspicion that Kitchin mocked at his taste for women with titles. When Kitchin was dying in Brighton, he repeatedly urged me to get Hartley to visit him. But although Neville Coghill, Lord David Cecil and Lord Ritchie, a former Chairman of the Stock Exchange, all came from farther away, and although Hartley had a comfortable car, with a chauffeur, in which to travel, there was always some excuse – Christobel Aberconway had invited him for the weekend, he was himself far from well, his chauffeur was "not all that keen" on long drives.

In a period long before the terms semantics and semiotics had become part of our literary jargon, Kitchin was fascinated by the nature of language, by words and meaning. This fascination declares itself at the outset of *Mr Balcony*, when Mr Balcony muses on words "both as symbols and as things-in-themselves", and then recalls how he once "repeated the word 'bed' over and over to himself and watched its dismantling – sheet after sheet, so to say, stripped off – till nothing was left but a pure sound ringing in my ears like a musical note, without associations".

At least in later life, when I knew him, Kitchin was always more of a listener than a talker, so that strangers, left to make the conversational running, would often complain of embarrassment and strain. But from time to time he would come out with something arrestingly witty or wise. Like all this books, *Mr Balcony* is full of such examples of his wit and his wisdom. "Long books are for those who haven't imagination enough to provide the padding." "If one has romantic notions, it is clear that one is unequal to their fulfilment." To attempt to fathom the character of one of the people in his novel is "like reading between the lines of a time-table".

On Kitchin's death I was telephoned by a reporter from the *Brighton Argus*, clearly in a high state of excitement. I was C.H.B. Kitchin's literary executor, was I not? I replied Yes. Then did I know that he had left three-quarters of a million? (This was when a million was worth twice what it is worth now). Again I replied Yes. "But none of us had any idea that such a famous writer was living in this town! That's almost as much money as Somerset Maugham left." I had to explain that Kitchin's money had come not from his books but from the wily investment of a number of inheritances.

Yet, in a sense, Brighton – like the rest of the world – had been in default. Contemporaries of far flimsier talent had attracted far more notice. The gods had showered both possessions and gifts on Clifford Kitchin – did not Leslie Hartley describe him as the most talented man that he had ever known? – but they had withheld from him the one thing that he most wanted: popularity. Perhaps the current reissue of some of his books will at long last bring that popularity to him. It is sadly overdue.

Francis King, London 1986

I

ST. VALENTINE'S DAY

MR. BALCONY's library, an L-shaped room on the first floor, which in any of the other houses in Lithe Street would have been called the drawing-room, was filled with brilliant sunshine. It was the 14th of February. Near the windows, on the writing-table, on the piano and on two little tables half covered with books and papers stood large pots of white hyacinths whose powerful scent lay heavily on the clear air. For the sake of the hyacinths the fire was not lit. "Indeed," thought Mr. Balcony, "they will live so long that I shall freeze to death."

He opened one of the French windows and stepped out on to the metal extension, a yard broad, which spanned the narrow frontage of the house :—" On to my namesake the balcony, in fact," he murmured, conscious both of his action and that his thoughts were settling down to a long paragraph. "There is no need, however, to be afraid of words," he continued. "They are, as I discovered some time ago, both symbols and things-in-themselves. I can still remember the day when I repeated 'bed' eight thousand times and watched its dismantling —sheet after sheet, so to say, stripped off—till nothing was left but a pure sound ringing in my ears like a musical note, without associations. Bed, bed, bed. As different from red or head in itself as are the objects symbolised by those sounds from one another. If only one could thus isolate the pure form of a whole language, expurgate a dictionary until a commonplace sentence like 'Will you shake the other end of that cylinder?' became meaningless—from the point of view of its translation into French. The impossibility of giving orders and receiving them might, to some, be a stumbling-block. 'At that rate,' they would say, 'why speak at all?'"

In the street a newspaper boy waved a

placard announcing races at Gatwick. Mr. Balcony from his perch replied with a gesture. The boy waved again, and the dual pantomime continued while Lady Hoobrake, returning from the post office, fumbled with the front-door of the next house.

" It is he," she thought, " who encourages the barrel-organs, and on New Year's Day detained a band of the unemployed for three hours." In appearance, he reminded her somewhat of the late Lord Kitchener when younger. " A figure inappropriate to those antics," she decided.

She went upstairs into the drawing-room, and found her son Aubrey playing a loud cadenza on the high notes of the piano.

" Wretch ! " she said, smoothing the powder on her nose with her third finger, " the telegram has cost me three and ninepence."

Aubrey did not answer, but when he had finished his exercise and his mother had resolved to make ready for luncheon rather than give him a piece of her mind, he rose and said, " I shall never go to Leighton's Cross again ! "

"Indeed, you have small chance of being invited, you good-for-nothing!"

"The first day there were billiards, and I cut the cloth. On the second, I was lent golf clubs and called them 'shooting-irons.' 'Boy,' he said, 'do you play no games?' 'None,' I said, 'but polo!' 'Then,' he said, 'we will ride and jump.' We rode, but before the first jump was reached, I fell."

"You have told me all this before, with different details."

"It is a good story. I want to practise it. That evening there was a party. No bridge, no poker, no dancing even, but rowdy round games, and a very rough hide-and-seek. I hid in my bedroom, but the door had no key, and three strong women dragged me downstairs by the ankles. My shirt was in tatters and my new blue silk vest lost two buttons. By accident I broke an old plate with a portrait of one of our ancestors in the middle. Uncle ffawkes, for whom I fear death by apoplexy, threw me into the cellar, where I lay in pain till everybody had gone to bed. The next day he gave me three pounds and that detestable introduction to Mr. Slicer."

" And after one day at the office, you turn up an hour late. To-day, you do not go at all. I wash my hands of you and your career."

" Wash your hands," he said, as the luncheon gong sounded. But his mother had already gone up a second flight of stairs for that purpose.

Three minutes later, the luncheon gong sounded in Mr. Balcony's house. Mr. Balcony left his cold library and without washing his hands went downstairs to his dining-room, where, waited upon by N'Gambi, his African servant, he ate a dozen oysters and an omelette.

On the ground floor of the last (or first) house in Lithe Street—at the junction of Lithe Street and Brompton Road—there was no gong to sound. Gloria Swing, senior partner in the *Maison Swing*, was eating a boiled egg and bread and butter in a sunless and untidy back-room, through the open door of which she could keep an eye on the door of the shop; for, after some argument with the landlord, the portion of the ground-floor facing the street had been converted into a shop-front. The morning had brought her no customers, even though, only the night before, she had taken everything out of the window except a biscuit-coloured cloche hat and a black evening gown, over which a girdle of little white bones wound in negligent coils. Even Mr. Balcony had not called.

She had made his treasured acquaintance the previous October, when she stocked knitted woollen goods and cigarettes. He had asked for matches and, finding none, had bought a pink and white striped jumper—undergraduate style, but broad in the chest. And, although on account of a tradesman's quarrel, she had abandoned tobacco and now dealt entirely in feminine wares, he rarely walked into the Brompton Road without bidding her good day.

His appeal to her grew as the influence of Mrs. O'Doyle decreased. To Mrs. O'Doyle she had owed her emancipation from Victorian rationalism, from the cult of organisms, survival values and the mechanics of nature. From

Mrs. O'Doyle she had learnt—having at the time a great appetite for such knowledge—that light was all about her, that an invisible world was beckoning under the coarse garb of common things to the enlightened eye. The spirits of Napoleon and Boadicea had appeared to her. " Steep," they said almost in verse, " is the path that you must tread, but radiance looms beyond the briars. Upwards, Gloria. Excelsior! Amen." And the end-feathers of the wings of her especial angel had more than once flickered across a roseate sky. But Mrs. O'Doyle had been too material a priestess. Her table-tapping ghosts talked gibberish or in such a vulgar vein that Gloria recoiled. The questions that Mrs. O'Doyle put to them were unworthy. She sought for guidance as to the coming weather and Derby winners, and once, with an eye to the business in which she was then a partner, asked whether waists that season were to move up or down. She also borrowed ten pounds from Gloria and was slow to repay. The partnership was severed after words.

It was in the dry period of failing faith that

Gloria met Mr. Balcony. From the first, his presence soothed her. On his third visit he gave her a sheet of foolscap, headed " Evils of Life." " Add to it, if you can," he said and left her to read it.

" The fear of death.
  Disease.
  The fear of disease.
  Unrequited love.
  Our unkindness to those we love.
  Unwelcome attentions.
  Faithlessness of friends.
  Misfortunes of friends.
  Triumph of enemies.
  Thwarted ambitions and dissatisfaction with oneself.
  Poverty.
  Innumerable minor vexations and discomforts which attend us every day, such as missing trains, being forced to hurry, petty physical exertions like shoe-lacing, buttoning, stooping and lifting heavy things.
  Fears and apprehensions of all kinds."

During the night she thought of many concrete examples, but of no new heading. When after a week he returned, he had forgotten about the list.

" But," she said, having reminded him of it,
" why did you write it ? "

" To justify myself, after the event."

" To justify ? "

" For caring for none of the contraries of
these things."

" But how ? " she began, and strove to read
the list in its converse sense—" the hope of life,
good health, the hope of good health," and so on.

" And what event ? " she said.

" Ah," he said, and fondled the sleeve of a
slightly soiled mink coat.

" Do you, then, want nothing ? "

" Yes, but not what you want—or as you
want it."

And he had left her, as if at the end of an
instalment of a detective story in serial form.

While Gloria, having eaten the egg, was
eating a digestive biscuit and still lamenting the
morning's solitude, Mr. Lace, who had an attic
in the house, and with his miserable savings had
bought Mrs. O'Doyle's share in the *Maison
Swing*, came in by a back-door.

" Busy ? " he asked, carefully placing his worn white muffler on a chair, on which thoughtlessly he afterwards sat.

" Not an order."

" In this fine weather, they go further afield."

" The quarter's profit, so far, is eighteen pounds."

" Including unpaid bills ? "

" Including them."

" Queen Eleanor is dead."

" So is Queen Anne."

" Eleanor, ex-queen. The memorial service gives me two columns. They almost sent me to Prague."

" Almost, almost——"

" Should you have liked me to go ? " he asked wistfully.

" I should feel less harassed if you earned something. For myself, I can just provide."

" Two columns."

" At what rate ? "

There was a noise on the stairs, and a door at the side of the house shut.

" The doctor," said Gloria.

" Is he ill again ? "

He was referring to Mr. Lloyd-Muce, who with his wife had the floor immediately over the shop. Gloria lived on the floor above them, and Mr. Lace on the top floor.

" He has no chance of recovering."

" Poor fellow. Hm, it's a race between us."

" Nonsense, Hilary."

" My cough is in its third week."

" You wrap your neck up too tightly."

" My doctor said there was danger of bronchitis."

" It isn't bronchitis that troubles Mr. Lloyd-Muce."

There was a pause, during which Mr. Lace was tormented by the black thoughts which rarely left him. Gloria gazed at the shop-door. " In this very respectable thoroughfare," she mused, " one can hardly expect adventure to come in to one."

Mr. Lace rose.

" I am going to rest," he said. " I shall be down at three."

He went upstairs, and the alarm-clock on the mantelpiece struck two.

Mr. Balcony finished his luncheon, walked upstairs and then down again, remembering a bunch of keys which he had left on the dining-room table. " What," he wondered, walking upstairs once more, " does it profit the universe that I should have to make two journeys to my library ? Are there actions which contribute nothing to the scheme of life ? Does the ' useless ' exist ? I have a suspicion that it does."

He stepped into the strong scent of the hyacinths.

" O exquisite fragrance ! How evident it is that the function of these bulbs is not only to propagate themselves and die, but, while they live, to be beautiful in themselves. Indeed, did they (or the life-force which engendered them) but know it, there is small chance of any further propagation by them of their species ; for I think I shall take longer to freeze to death than they to wither. And, once withered, the dust-bin for them."

He opened his desk, took some papers from a pigeon-hole and made calculations in pencil, first on the back of an old envelope and then on a sheet of new note-paper. Round the address, " 38, Lithe Street, S.W.," he drew a scroll which might have decorated a memorial tablet in a cathedral. And instantly he thought of a cathedral, musty with the incense of shut windows, while the colours of the county battalion hung motionless from a long pole, and in a loft overhead the organist's daughter spelt out with erring feet the subject of a Bach fugue. There was an enchanting peace in the contemplation of English ecclesiasticism, ascetic, yet luxuriant with choirmasters and precentors—Stanford in E flat, Dykes in F. Was there not a canon's wife who said she had played roulette in the crypt—while her husband, no doubt, wandered with an umbrella beneath the desolate elms, contented, and vaguely sensual ? February was the month of the cathedral town.

February to June was four months. By that time Brompton Road would have assumed a festive air, and of an evening young couples without hats would float westwards on the bus tops.

"In June," he murmured. "No more Decembers, with the pneumonia patient breathing in the fog—— Let it be June."

He made further calculations and pencil drawings, and then, throwing the papers into the waste-paper basket, rose, bent over the nearest hyacinths, straightened himself, and went downstairs quietly, in accordance with a past habit; for there had been a time when self-consciousness made him unwilling that the servants should know when he came in or out.

In the hall he rang a bell. N'Gambi came up from the basement, helped him on with his fur coat and gave him his top-hat and umbrella. They had a short conversation in a foreign tongue, and Mr. Balcony, feeling for keys and silver in his left and right trouser pockets respectively, went out into Lithe Street and walked past Nos. 36 to 2, even numbers. When he came to No. 2, the corner house, whose address the landlord had for years tried in vain to have altered to a number in Brompton Road, despite the clear intention of the architect to build in Lithe Street, he paused, wondering whether to go inside and visit Gloria or not. He had no definite impulse either way.

"If I cannot decide," he thought, "hunger will drive me home again before night. But if I do stand here, it will be of no great moment."

Gloria, a toque in either hand and another held in her teeth by the edge, appeared in the window and beckoned him inside. He shook his head mournfully, smiled and framed the words, "Alas, to-day it cannot be."

As he passed, she gazed wistfully, and then put down her burdens. "There are days," she thought, "on which one longs for a piece of good and unexpected news. This is one of them." She remembered home-comings at the end of summer holidays, the damp smell of the house that she seemed never to have left, the disappointment of a pile of letters in which the good news should have lain. But there was no good news. An artist had ventured to leave, for approval, a portfolio of pictures, prices on back.

23

" The occupier " was invited to learn revolver shooting in preparation for the street fighting which would follow the November strike. On note of hand money would be lent.

" You drift," Mrs. O'Doyle had said censoriously, " expecting somebody or some event outside you, to give you happiness. Happiness is within you. Seek it there."

" A piece of good news," thought Gloria, as she arranged the hats in the window.

By a side-door—the house was full of doors, each with its purpose—Mrs. Lloyd-Muce, chin in air, walked out into Lithe Street. Gloria divined her errand.

" She is going," she said to herself, " to the chemist to get the medicine which the doctor prescribed for her husband this morning. She is thinking, ' Will it be long ? I must set the teeth and grin.' How she steps out, chin in air, braving the vision of the death-bed—a true *family-girl*."

She laughed gently. *Family-girl*. It was the pink Swede from Gothenburg who had said of a Duke's daughter, ' It is visible that she is a true *family-girl*.' And when someone had looked puzzled and others tittered, he explained the derivation—*familjeflicka*, and the rest of it. "Is it not a reasonable *transference*? Have you not the word?" he had asked. "In the matter of fisheries, we find Norway a *difficult concurrent*," was another of his observations. Mr. Lace had been there, taking notes for an article to be called "Foreigners and English," or—if a weekly would accept it—"The Nature of Idiom." "Words have more meaning in their associations, than they have in themselves," was part of his thesis. "Therefore, if one is a foreigner and does not know the associations"—and so on.

The shop-door opened. Gloria rose from her cramped position in the window and turned round to greet the visitor. It was not a customer but Mrs. O'Doyle. When Mrs. O'Doyle and Gloria dissolved partnership, Mrs. O'Doyle had said, as people usually do when they know that a friendship is over, "I hope it will make no difference to our excellent relationship. We must always keep in touch." To keep in touch, she called once in every six weeks. She was this time a little overdue.

" Love-sick, my dear ? " she asked with a disparaging glance.

" Rubbish, Juliana. You know I've had enough of that."

They went into the back-room and sat down, Mrs. O'Doyle in a wicker arm-chair, and Gloria in the hard chair opposite the remains of her luncheon, still negligently there.

" None the less, Gloria, a man's coming into your life."

" Two or three are already in it, Juliana."

" This fine day, you oughtn't to be sitting in. Last night, Rosabel and I did the *grand jeu*. Eight packs and three hours before it came out. I questioned about you. How's trade ? "

" There isn't any."

Mrs. O'Doyle nodded with satisfaction.

" I thought not. Now Rosabel and I made forty pounds last week. But that's by the way. You're doing no good, the cards said, and won't do any. But there was a man in the cards, not exactly a nice man, I'm afraid, who was coming after you. Can you think of no man, my dear ? Oh, don't bamboozle me with your ' two or three.' I flatter myself I know when a man's a man with you, or any woman. Is there none?"

"I wish there were," said Gloria defensively.

"Well, you're to have your wish—and you'll go a journey with him, probably by boat, and after that——"

"We shall settle down in a house with trees round it," said Gloria, quoting rudely a familiar past prophecy.

"No, there were no trees. Or, rather, there were, but not round a house."

"What a change."

Mrs. O'Doyle patted Gloria's hand.

"No wonder you're out of sorts, my dear, with business as sluggish as a colonel's liver. But haven't I told you, you can't flourish here with Harrod's against you—and the windows not even looking into Brompton Road? A shop in a residential street—unless you've a connection —can't prosper. Soho's very different. We've got the floor above now, and another ten tables. Last night we had dancing; to-morrow we're having duets on the banjulele. But this is by the way. Come out, my dear, and walk in the winds.

Let the men in the park see your skirt swirling round those pretty knees of yours."

" I can't leave the shop yet. Lace isn't on duty for another half-hour."

" Of course, if you're expecting a customer, now——"

Gloria took an unpaid bill from a file on the table, and wrote on the back in block capitals :

DAMN YOU ! I'VE WAITED FOR YOU ALL THE MORNING. WE OPEN AGAIN AT HALF-PAST THREE.

" That'll do fine," said Mrs. O'Doyle.

" Perhaps though, I'd better tear some of it off."

" No. Leave it. Serve them right."

Gloria tore off the first nine words, put on her hat and coat, fastened the notice to the shop-door, which she locked, and set out with Mrs. O'Doyle for Kensington Gardens.

Mr. Balcony had reached Paley's Court, a turning in Throgmorton Street. He went into a doorway and up two flights of stairs which circled round the lift. As he went up, the lift went down. "If we could exchange bodies with one another when we wished," he thought, "what time we should save. Indeed, we should hardly have to move at all; for, wherever I go, I find someone going in the opposite direction."

He opened a glass door with HEAVENS & SLICER printed upon it in gold letters.

"Mr. Slicer?"

"Name, please?" asked an office-boy, sitting by a tape machine, from which a strand of paper fell into a waste-paper basket.

"So every moment is an excitement to you," said Mr. Balcony, patting the boy on the head with the handle of his umbrella, while his right hand brought the latest price of Berengarias nearer to his eyes.

"Steady on, sir! What name shall I say?"

"Balcony."

"Balcony?"

"I suppose you hear, but you don't understand."

"Sorry, sir, I'm new to this job."

"I have no doubt that in a short time it

will become distressingly familiar to you," Mr. Balcony murmured, as the boy flung himself exuberantly into the inner office. "Routine will get you—by the seat of your trousers." And he surveyed pensively the empty stool.

The boy, after a few moments, came back and led him into a cubicle with glass walls, frosted up to the height of bald heads bent over ledgers in the adjoining cubicles, but, above that, clear till the ceiling. Seated, one had privacy; standing, the sensation of living in a honeycomb. Thought, in that environment, took upon itself a brittle and deceptive clarity.

Mr. Slicer, on account of a slight squint, and jerky habits of gesture, was by his friends described as "a real Dickens type." "You will," they used to add, "not find his like again in a million."

After an exchange of compliments Mr. Balcony drew a list from his pocket, and said, "Will you please sell these to-day?" Mr. Slicer read the list, making full display of all his characteristics and demurred.

"Berengarias are talked to eight," he said.

" The report is due in a fortnight. Would you not care to wait ? "

" They have certainly risen to thirty shillings since you suggested I should exchange into Lucky Dips," answered Mr. Balcony, but I see no further prospects for them."

" As for that Lucky Dips are stronger to-day."

" With the commodity."

" And for these," said Mr. Slicer, indicating an item with his thumb, " there is said to be a fine future."

" Sell."

" And the Hedgehog Debentures, which mature in August ? We shall not get more than 99⅝ for them. The situation is clouded by a monetary stringency."

" August is too late. Sell. I have not included my holding in Argentina Conveyers, redeemable in March."

" Unfortunately, they will not be redeemed."

" How so ? "

Mr. Slicer explained.

" But," he said, " you must have had the notice."

"Probably. I have either forgotten, or did not read it."

"Indeed, you mystify me, Mr. Balcony. You give an impression of such acumen, you show such general knowledge. You are the only client of whom I am afraid."

"I have the jargon. That is all. Sell, then, my Argentina Conveyers. £800.

"They stand at only 72."

"Half a loaf."

"Well, there's sense in that. And now, as to reinvestment. Would you entertain, as a sweetener, some Lucky Dips?"

"I shall not reinvest."

"Oh, Mr. Balcony! This is indeed a knock-out."

"On deposit, money earns three per cent."

"It is thought that the rate will go down."

"And the monetary stringency?"

"True—for the moment. But, taking the long view, you may not be able to reinvest without loss. And with money on deposit there is always the temptation to nibble at capital, to commit financial sacrilege."

" I shall invest no more."

" Alas," said Mr. Slicer, profiting by a look of abstraction on Mr. Balcony's face, and assuming an eloquence which he thought might be agreeable to his client, " is this the end? Are we to say good-bye? Will you visit us no more, as you used to, amaze us no more with your spectacular ill-fortune, and your incomprehensible strokes of luck? Have you the heart to forsake us? "

" It is," said Mr. Balcony, " good-bye."

As he went out, he gave the boy in the outer office a bulging envelope.

" Here," he said, " is a bearer certificate for ten shares of ten Mexican dollars each in the Splendid and Universal Oilfields Limited. They pay no dividend, and their present value is three-farthings, buyers. Watch them well. They may be the seeds of your fortune. The gambler's curse be upon you."

And before comment was possible, he had gone.

The busy streets were so full of people that it seemed hardly possible that each one should have a separate personality. They wandered and hurried this way and that, now turning abruptly sideways, now revolving, sometimes casting glances in all directions, sometimes doggedly intent on sky or pavement.

As Mr. Balcony threaded his way through the living maze he was reminded of a walk which he had taken, a few days after he had first come to London, with a friend older than himself who had since died.

" You see all these people," the friend had said. " Do you not hate them ? "

The idea of hatred uncaused by personal injury was then new to Mr. Balcony, and shocked him.

" What have they done to me ? " he asked.

" They are our enemy, the crowd," said his companion, " life's mass production, the spawn of that monstrous fish, humanity. They shout with one voice, act with one purpose, see with one vision. And they will have none who differ from them. If by touching this grating with your stick you could annihilate them all, would you not do so?"

"They are the bees," Mr. Balcony had answered, "who make my honey."

He passed the door of one of the hundred "Tyger's Tea Rooms" in London. Within, the white caps of the waitresses twinkled like stars. People streamed in and out. It was a company in which he had had shares. "Until a few moments ago," he reflected, "the pennies in the pockets of these people went to pay me. It was on my behalf that these nimble waitresses presented their pink bills. These vans, full of rolls and ice-bricks, sped the streets for me. If they delayed my taxi, I comforted myself with the thought of fine trade. Now it is nothing to me, and if London prefers to starve, it is at the expense of others."

After the tea-shop came a hosier's, then a tobacconist's, then a chemist's, in all of which he had been interested; for he had held an unusual proportion of industrial shares. But if London still wore Box's shilling ties, smoked Pipely's mixture, and purged itself with Dredger's laxative, it concerned him no longer.

On reaching the north end of Kingsway, Mr. Balcony followed the crowd into Holborn tube station. Four lifts went down before he entered one, and the officials chuckled together over his absent - mindedness. " It shows," thought Mr. Balcony, whom little escaped, " how different are our standards. These fellows can conceive of no more urgent need than that of changing one's geographical situation. If I asked them why my thoughts were necessarily of less value to me than the speed with which I am to reach home, they would be puzzled."

His neighbour in the lift was Aubrey Hoobrake, with whom, since the time when he had demanded a personal apology for a burst of piano-playing at three o'clock in the morning, he was slightly acquainted.

" Hello ! " said Aubrey.

They settled side by side in a smoking compartment.

"I have been to my stockbroker's," said Mr. Balcony, with generous abandonment of reserve.

"Heavens & Slicer? I know them."

"You? Was it yours, the stool near the door?"

"Another one, upstairs. I went the day before yesterday, with excellent introductions to Mr. Slicer. Given industry, a partnership was in sight. I saw your name in a ledger."

"Then why are you not there now? The working day is not yet over."

"Yesterday, I was an hour late. There was a great unpleasantness."

"Mr. Slicer, I suppose, has two voices—one for me and one for you."

"He has a very loud voice. This morning, on waking, I had an inhibition. I could not go at all. Ten o'clock once in a lifetime is enough, don't you think? 'Ten to-day,' I said to myself, 'and ten to-morrow. Nothing achieved, and ten the day after. A thousand days from to-day, and still ten o'clock.'"

"It may be a Sunday."

"It isn't. I've worked it out. Ten years from to-day, and still ten o'clock. It is like putting on your shoes. No amount of careful lacing one day will put them on the next. Like cleaning your teeth. However well you brush them to-day, you will have to brush them to-morrow. And in the end they'll decay and come out. So this morning I didn't go at all. My mother sent a long and misleading telegram, and forced me to go up this afternoon. 'In case you lose touch,' she said, 'you must go this afternoon. Perhaps they won't want you to-morrow.' But they will, they will."

His eyes filled with tears.

"And this afternoon?" Mr. Balcony asked firmly.

"This afternoon I got as far as the Bank, and had another inhibition. I loitered for half an hour, and here I am."

"It is the most romantic of all careers, for those who, like yourself, are not bothered by a social conscience. Even the typists have their little gambles. There is much behind those ledgers."

" I have no capital to gamble with. All I had to do was to add up a column of figures. I can't add. I won't go again."

" The only way not to go again," suggested Mr. Balcony, " is to write and post a rude letter. That would make it impossible."

" A marvellous idea ! "

Mr. Balcony felt in his pocket and pulled out a letter card, and gave it to Aubrey.

" Can you write on this newspaper ? "

" Yes."

" Then write this, ' 36, Lithe Street, Brompton Road, S.W. Dear Sir—My experience of your office and the way in which your business is conducted has given me such a distaste for your society and the career on which I was under your auspices to embark, that I have decided on no account ever to set foot in Paley's Court again. The traffic in stocks and shares seems to me to be a low and contemptible occupation which no decent-minded man or woman can practise without shame. Yours truly.' Then your name."

" Perhaps," said Aubrey, " this is going rather far."

" If you want half-measures, seek no advice from me."

" You must feel pretty strongly about it. Have you had bad luck ? "

" I ? "

" I beg your pardon, sir."

" Seal it, boy, and address it, and post it on leaving the tube."

For a few minutes they were silent. Then Mr. Balcony said :

" I should not like you to think in the least that I subscribe to any of the sentiments in your letter. I still think that the profession of stock-broker is, apart from the army, the finest profession for any young man. I was merely giving expression to your own feelings. If you have any doubts whatsoever tear up the letter at once, and leave it among the cigarette ends on the floor. I added the ethical claptrap to make the breach unbridgeable ; for nothing else will rankle so deeply with Mr. Slicer. Naturally, I do not suppose you to possess a social conscience."

" And why not, Mr. Balcony ? "

" People who realise the fatigue of dressing

and undressing, of the daily and unproductive routine of life, as you do, have no emotions to spare for humanity. The humanitarian—I might almost say 'your' humanitarian, since 'your' is an adjective of great offensive power, as in the phrase 'Read your Brontës,' when you have read nothing by those authors—your humanitarian, I was saying, is nearly always personally insensitive. He tolerates dirt and bad smells. He has no taste in food, or drink, or dress. He only resents insincerity when it conflicts with his own point of view. Finding no resource or inspiration in himself, he goes for it to the crowd. He battens on a mass-idealism. He calls selfish those who are more self-sufficient."

" So you think," asked Aubrey, who had been thinking but not listening, " that I might do worse ? "

" I do. Of course, you do not perhaps realise the full effect of office life. Nothing is more quickly fatal to the youthful bloom. In a few weeks your complexion, of which I can see you are proud, will be pale and pasty. In a few months you will grow fat, or anæmic and skinny. You are not one, I fear, to keep yourself fit with exercise, indoor or outdoor. You will also find your manner changing. It will become both 'smart' and furtive. Hang - dog one moment, you will force yourself into a cheeky cockney vitality the next. You will have the air of one who knows a thing or two, of the 'live-wire' in embryo. You will become vulgar, in mind and body. This is of course nothing of great moment. It equips one well for the battle of life. You will be like the son of a former friend of mine, who came back from the war and said to me one Easter Day, 'It's rum, isn't it, to think that six years ago *I* used to get up at five and put on a cassock and serve at Mass every morning?' There was a quality in his pronunciation of the personal pronoun, which did not recommend him to me. But these are matters for your own intelligence, if it is sufficient to grapple with them."

Aubrey sighed and looked at the fresco of advertisements adorning the compartment.

" You vacillate," said Mr. Balcony. " Destroy the letter." But when, being minded to walk a little, they got out at Knightsbridge, Aubrey posted it in the first pillar-box he saw.

Meanwhile, Gloria and Mrs. O'Doyle had taken their walk in the park, and at the end of it had fallen in with Major O'Hoone, an old crony of Mrs. O'Doyle's and descended from rival kings. He had proposed to entertain the ladies to tea at one of Tyger's Tea Rooms, where they spent a garrulous half-hour. The Major's incessant compliments and Mrs. O'Doyle's innuendoes provoked Gloria to a display of artificiality. She indulged in fantastic sallies, and the Major laughed at all of them. Some really amused him; by others he was mystified. But when he failed to understand he laughed the louder.

"I feel," Gloria thought, "like a nursemaid in 1900 who has met a red-coated soldier, when wheeling baby by the Albert Memorial, and goes home to a shrimp tea with Tom and Florrie in the basement, chaste but saucy."

"And a dark man's coming into your life," crooned Mrs. O'Doyle.

" At a place with trees round it."

" Maybe they were not exactly trees."

" Men as trees walking."

" What about the park, anyway ? " asked the Major with a wink.

" 'Gainst fate," sang Mrs. O'Doyle, " 'Gainst fate, can no maid strugg-ugg-uggle."

" How many children then ? "

" Why, my love, as many as you wish. That's not a matter of fate these days.

> " There was an old woman,
>   Who lived in a shoe.
>   She hadn't any children,
>   Because——"

" Sh ! "

" Well, I dare say, your fertile imagination can complete the ditty."

" The manageress thinks us abandoned, I fear."

" Ouf, the smug respectability of Kensington. If I had my way, they'd learn a thing or two."

At Mrs. O'Doyle's raised voice a dozen customers looked round.

44

" Well, here's another balmy day come to an end," said the Major.

" I should like to spend the twilight gathering cowslips in an immense meadow, stretching down to the sea. When it got quite dark, a little rowing-boat would come out of the mist, and take me home."

" Tut, tut ! What a fancy ! "

" And when we had gone a short way from the shore, someone would run to the water's edge, and call for me in a sing-song voice. And I should sit trailing one hand over the side of the boat trying to catch a bottle bobbing up and down in the water, and say nothing."

" And what a state they'd all be in, by Jove ! "

" They would say," she pursued, " 'at any rate, her life is insured for a hundred thousand pounds !' And the next morning they would all walk solemnly through the cowslips I hadn't picked to the beach, and look very silly as they clambered amongst the rocks and slipped on the sticky seaweed."

" But, my darling Gloria, why aren't you writing it all down and sending it to some paper? I'm sure you'd earn a better living by your pen than by your present business."

"Are you a fortune-teller?" Major O'Hoone asked.

"No. I'm a milliner."

"There's another one hasn't heard of the *Maison Swing*," said Mrs. O'Doyle, not without a chuckle. "Give it up, my dear, and join me, or better still——" And she whispered something in Gloria's ear.

A waitress came up to the table, her vivacious eyes belying the demureness of her features, and gave the Major a pink bill with a gesture which invited him to pat her hand. Had the conversation maintained the boisterous quality of its opening, he would have done so.

Instead, he felt in an inside pocket, and then, puckering his brow, in all his other pockets.

"Damn it all!" he said.

"No accident, I hope," said Mrs. O'Doyle.

A search in his left trouser pocket yielded one halfpenny.

"Knew I was out of small change. But, note-case, note-case . . . Can't find note-case."

46

" Probably you've left it at home, between the hair-wash and the shaving-brush."

" 'Pon my word, it's too bad. How can I apologise to you, ladies ? Here, waitress, take my card to the manageress, will you ? "

" Good heavens!" said Mrs. O'Doyle, " and the bill's only one and eightpence. Surely 'tis almost paid as it is. Gloria, darling, pay the girl before there's more ado. I've nothing on me."

Gloria paid.

When her companions had left her, she walked slowly along Knightsbridge and Brompton Road. The pale sun was setting, and the western sky was full of yellowish light. In front of her, hardly more than thirty paces in front of her, walked Mr. Balcony and Aubrey. She quickened her step and then resumed her slow gait.

" Every day," she thought, " it becomes lighter. We shall have spring, then summer, light, more light and warmth, stronger colours, stronger feelings." She pictured the sun growing daily fiercer and larger, stabbing the quivering air with bright rays, piercing the young leaves and covering the ground with brilliant points of light, while in soft layers vapours rose upwards from the earth, becoming, the higher they went, thinner, more rarefied and extended. It was to her the progress of an ecstasy. " Let there be an end," she willed, " of crawling about in darkness past rows of dripping arc-lamps, gliding like a ghost through the fog, trudging through snow and slush and slime. Let us begin with spring and end with summer, burnt to the bone!"

A man with one leg held out a bunch of violets and snowdrops. She gave him sixpence. But the flowers had no scent and wetted the tip of her nose.

Mr. Balcony had increased his lead, and she hurried to lessen it. The corner of Lithe Street and her shop beneath the arc-lamp came into view. As she crossed the road, she saw him stop and look in at the window. No doubt, Mr. Lace was there, busy with his spectacles, his writing-pad or his thick novel. The length of these classics, she thought. A year's undertaking to read a single one. Long books are for those

48

who haven't imagination enough to provide the padding.

She reached her door. Mr. Balcony was still by the window, though Aubrey, whom she now recognised, was plainly, by his detached movement, impatient of the delay. She came up with boldness.

" Can I serve you, sir ? "

He looked round and nodded.

" I like that little hat. Why don't you wear it ? "

" It is," she said, " for those who go to Cowes —a yachting hat."

" Then," said Aubrey, who could never conceal his knowledge of women's clothes, " you have put it out too early in the year. Besides, I shouldn't call it a yachting hat at all. It's the kind worn by women who are spending Easter in Paris at someone else's expense — and wish to look as if they are going farther afield. I've seen them, at Victoria."

" At any rate, it's spring-like."

" How much is it ? "

" Three guineas."

" Too much, you know."

" Be off with you, sir," said Mr. Balcony
suddenly.

Aubrey bent his head in dejection.

" When I think," he said, " of all the bother,
the fuss, the explanations to-morrow morning,
my mother sitting at the writing-table, dabbing
her eyes with the pen-wiper; for she is short-
sighted——"

" I help those who can help themselves.
Away with you."

And with his umbrella he gave a smart cut at
Aubrey's legs.

Aubrey went without protest, trying not to
let it be seen that he had noticed the blow. Mr.
Balcony and Gloria were left alone.

" It has been," she said, " a lovely day."
" A lovely day," she repeated, looking at a
huge tawny cloud beneath which the sun had
dropped.

" Now it is over."

" Won't you come inside—for a cocktail ? "
she asked.

" Thank you, but not to-night."

"Mr. Lace is there," she said, as if to reassure him.

"Yes, I suppose so."

He turned round, waved his hand, struck the air with his umbrella as if beheading a dandelion or aiming at another pair of legs, and walked slowly up the street. Gloria unlocked the door and went inside. "Complaining of his cough and leaves the window open," she thought, going upstairs, and seeing Mr. Lace, sitting with a book in the back-room, as she had pictured him. She was to go with him to the theatre that night. As a journalist he often had free seats. She sank on to her bed with a feeling of exhaustion, and shut her eyes. A clear and fastidious voice floated up from the street and through the open window.

"Then she asked me about his people," the voice said, "and it was really rather awkward. I told her they were very nice in an old-fashioned way—the father full of the footpath committee, and the mother on the *qui vive* about the apple sauce and the door into the yard which someone had left open. . . ."

The speaker passed.

Cold air came through the window, and the end of the blind flapped in a rising breeze. She went to the window and shut it. The arc-lamps flared steadily, undimmed by daylight. " Mauve or apricot?" she wondered, on her bed once more. "What, anyway, is there to dress up for? Half-a-dozen journalists with ill-fitting soft collars coming up in the interval. ' Hello, Lace! Ah! Miss Swing! Glad to see you, Miss Swing!' Pale, ugly intellectual faces. And their women, so advanced and so common. It is obvious to all the stalls that we're not at the theatre in our own right—that we're there for business, not pleasure. Mr., Mrs. and Miss Plate, and young Freddie Aspirol. ' I like a play with some legs in it,' says Mr. Plate. ' And what do you like, Daisy?' ' Less talk and more doing, Fred.' But even that is better than ' dramatic values,' and ' implied arguments.'

" Between the Acts. Grieg on the orchestra. ' Shall we go to the foyer? Cigarette?' ' No thank you, no lemonade, no ice, no chocolates.' ' Hello, Bamie!' ' What a draught! My cough, in its third week.' Curtain. Author. ' Thank you all for your kind er—er—er.' A clumsy bow. ' Such a mean-looking little man.' A pale, ugly, intellectual face. The commissionaire by the door knows we have no tip for him. Besides he is busy with Mrs. Plate. ' A bus then? The tube?' ' Oh, this rain, and my cough, my cough!' ' Why didn't you bring goloshes then?' ' A man can't . . .' "

There was a sound from the room below of something falling. A chair, perhaps, littered with papers, a bed-jacket, and the new medicine that Mrs. Lloyd-Muce had fetched that day from the chemist's? Another night to be faced by them both. "Don't go, Anna! Don't leave me!" Night and long wakefulness on the hard bed. Dreams, feverishness. Mrs. Lloyd-Muce, throwing back her head, grinning and bearing. Oh, hateful night, hateful winter! . . .

The sun shines on the rocks, gently at first, then more violently. The receding tide licks the seaweed, which frizzles and gives out a strong sea-smell. The smell gathers, forms into a whitish-yellow cloud, and rises, drawn out by the sun, from the shore like matter from a boil. One forgets oneself, and tickles one's bare feet by rubbing them against the burning rock. A little boat splashes through the surf, and a bottle bobs up and down by its side. . . .

She slept, and woke at Mr. Lace's weak, but impatient, knock.

"Lucima says dinner's cold, dear."

"What?"

"Dinner's ready. Are you?"

"Me? Good God! No. Begin. Fell asleep."

Gloria dressed, went downstairs, ate hurriedly a bad dinner, and went with Mr. Lace to the play. The rest of her evening was just as she had imagined it.

Aubrey and his mother had dinner alone together. With his evening clothes he wore a soft silk shirt and an enormous black satin bow-tie, and she a dress covered with metal ornaments which fitted like a coat of mail round her large bosom. With the soup, a green watery soup containing large slices of almost raw carrot, came the first embarrassing question.

"And how did business go to-day, Aubrey?"

He parried it, and others, guiltily.

"This Mr. Slicer," his mother went on, "seems a hard man. But you must bear with him, Aubrey. Thanks to Uncle ffawkes's protection, you are sure of a partnership in a few weeks. Then, of course, you can do as you please. When have you to go to-morrow?"

"To-morrow—I haven't to go."

"Do they keep holiday, then?"

Aubrey could not assent to this. His mother might easily have the wit to notice the financial column in the *Morning Post* and draw her own conclusion.

"No," he said, "but they won't want me to-morrow."

During the fish, skinny lemon sole curled into a pyramid and covered with a tepid white paste, he had leisure to reflect upon the great truthfulness of his reply.

"Lady Rumbleholm's son is making a thousand pounds a year and he is only twenty-three. Clive Westerley married at twenty-four and has a charming house—and twins. And Henry Lend—I forget what he's doing, but he's doing very well. Stockbrokers all. No mutton, dear?"

"We had beef at luncheon. I can't bear meat twice a day."

"But it was only cold beef."

"I know, there was nothing else. I had to eat it to keep up my strength."

During the sweet they talked of food, but with dessert, when the servant had left the room, Aubrey had to bear fresh probes.

"And what did you say to Mr. Slicer? You haven't told me."

"I referred to my experience of his office, and the way in which his business was conducted."

"Oh! Was that quite tactful?"

"And I said I shouldn't go again."

"Aubrey! Can I believe my ears?"

"Yes, you can," he said rudely, pushed the figs away and went upstairs to the piano.

His mother followed, but as soon as she began

to expostulate, he darted through the door, put on his hat and coat, and went to the house of a friend, who, he knew, would be having an evening's poker. His mother, after many bitter thoughts, went to her uncomfortable writing table, littered with photographs, vases and paper-weights, and wrote a long letter to her brother, General ffawkes Harrier. She then took up Michael Arlen's latest, but had no heart for it. Aubrey came back the poorer by two pounds long after she had gone to bed.

Mr. Balcony had three letters to write, and wrote them while Lady Hoobrake was writing hers. She did not realise that only a thin panel of brick and plaster separated her from the source of her vexation. But he was the first to finish, and after taking a turn in his cold room—for the hyacinths still made a fire impossible—he unlocked a drawer that served as base to one of his book-cases, and pulled out some piles of manuscript, tied up in red tape.

Then he sat down in an arm-chair, undid the tape, and looked carelessly through the first six bundles, laying them on one side as he finished them. The seventh, however, he read less quickly. It was as follows :

"Till I was twenty, the task of adapting myself to the rules which, for what reason I know not, seemed to govern my life, had been so weighty that I had had small leisure to regard myself as a person at all, as a being with aptitudes and deficiencies, and still less as a being with likes and dislikes. But there came a time, when more and more clearly, I saw myself as I had been, remembered various humiliations and successes, such as those which I have already recorded, and saw them not only in a fairer perspective, but in their relation to that unchanged part of me which perhaps wrongly I call 'myself.' The picture of 'myself' was not exhilarating. 'But,' I thought, 'in a short time, all will be very different. I shall develop, somehow, an authority. Instead of studying the caprices of others, others will study mine. My opinions will be accepted as the fruits of experience'—'experience of what ?' I might have asked myself, but I did not —'instead of arousing contempt or irritation.

Above all, I have passed the days of hand-to-hand fighting, the mêlée. . . .'

"It was with a shock, therefore, that I compared myself with my uncle Louis and the Professor. The wretchedness of their lives had so strongly impressed me, that to think of myself as growing in their images, filled me with dismay. My little conflicts with them, previously described, had blinded me to the kinship of my nature with theirs. Now that they were both dead, and I could consider them without being troubled by the discomfort which I had always felt in their society, I saw every day more distinctly how they came to be what they were, why neither of them had been able (in G.'s phrase) ' to come to terms with life,' and how impossible it was that I should avoid following in their footsteps.

"My confidence in the future changed to distrust. With my two patterns before me, I imagined myself as I should be ten or twenty years later. In the Professor I had a model of an injudicious marriage. I foresaw a considerable trial of family life, the formation of irksome ties which I should have no courage to break—the strangeness of manner which I should acquire through continual self-suppression, the titters of my wife's friends, the pity of my own, the weakness with which, whenever I was compelled to do anything, I should do myself an ill turn, and in the end, inevitable catastrophe.

"Uncle Louis, on the other hand, warned me against a horrible celibacy. Well I remembered the figure of fun which we had chosen to make him, the docility with which, for the sake of peace, he would play the buffoon, his sudden efforts to stand on his dignity, our contempt of his erudition, the meanness of my father's jealousy. 'You will grow,' I told myself, 'into an ineffectual old man—you will lose your hair and your teeth, and suffer secretly from a thousand small physical degradations. Picture yourself with your bland and foolish figure, going about the business of life. "Oh," they will say, "it's only Uncle Felix. He means well. Between ourselves, of course. . . ." And they will shrug their shoulders and think you notice nothing. And you will grow still older, and when the fatal illness comes, you will know what feelings they hide beneath their fitful solicitude.'

" At this period, too, I had morbid fears of my own health and could not believe, that having inherited my uncle's money, I should not perhaps inherit more than that. . . ."

Here Mr. Balcony with some impatience turned over two or three pages.

" One afternoon in May of the same year, I went to a large tea-party given by Mrs. L., when I met a very beautiful woman. She wore, I remember, exquisite clothes, and carried a big bunch of orchids tied up in grey satin ribbon. The charm of her manner entranced me. We had a long conversation, and I was grateful to her for the ease which I felt while I talked to her ; for I was almost a stranger at the L.'s, and had little self-assurance amongst those whom I did not know well. When at last she rose to go, I ventured to hope that it would not be long before I saw her again. She smiled at me for a moment, and then, with hardly a tremor in her voice, said,

' Good-bye. I am going to-night to a nursing-home, to have an operation from which I do not think I shall recover.' Before I had time to say anything in reply, she went out of the room, and I was too timid to follow her. I heard afterwards that she died in great pain a few days later.

" It was on that day that I first conceived the idea of altering my character, of doing violence to myself, and being all that nature had not intended me to be, and nothing that she had. But, for the time, the means of producing such a change perplexed me.

" *Note* 1.—When I speak of ' nature,' I may be held to be in a philosophical confusion. In one sense, of course, nature intends us to be whatever we are. *E.g.* If one is naturally inclined to be a sluggard, and by dint of practice succeeds in rising every day at dawn, one cannot say ' I am now an early riser—I have thwarted nature,' for the fact of one's wishing not to be a sluggard is also in nature, and early rising is afterwards as natural to one as long hours in bed used once to be. I do not use ' nature ' in such a wide sense, but rather refer it to an accumulation of personal habits in a fixed environment. Thus, at the age of which I am speaking, I saw that, given no sudden twist, my life would follow that of the Professor or my uncle Louis. I had, however, the force of their examples, which they had not. An acorn that falls on poor soil and takes root, will grow in a certain manner. But it is possible to transplant the little tree.

" *Note* 2.—As for the ' intentions ' of nature, I have never set much store by any personification, such as the words might imply. The stimulus, however, of thwarting an imaginary foe——"

Here, in the middle of a sentence, Mr. Balcony yawned, rose from his chair, and threw as much of the manuscript as he had read into the waste-paper basket, without troubling to tear it up. In due course it was cast with other rubbish into the dust-bin, and no one ever saw it again.

Then, hearing ten o'clock strike, he went up to his bedroom, stripped and spent a strenuous hour doing physical exercises, after which he put on his pyjamas, got into bed, and fell almost immediately asleep.

II

THE PROCESSION

GLORIA awoke at a quarter-past seven, sprang
from her bed, went into the bathroom at the
back, into which between two formidable houses
poured a flood of April sunshine, and lit the
geyser. While the water was boiling, she went
to the window, and scanned anxiously the little
patch of sky that was visible to her. It was of a
brilliant blue, and cloudless. The ripple of an
easterly wind moved the curtain. " Set fair,
set fair," she thought. " With this wind, no
rain. And on the other side of the house we shall
be sheltered. Nature is too kind."

Humming a little air, and full of joy, she threw
off her dressing-gown and pyjamas and posed on
one leg in front of the long mirror, whose presence in the bathroom had amazed the decorators.

" Roughly speaking, flawless," she said to herself, as she saw her image in the glass. " Small, perhaps, but vigorous—what do they say?— *garçonne*—the figure *à la mode*. No features, that's a pity, but a pleasant, willing expression. And a neat little head of hair, fitting close like an aeroplane hat." There was a patch of sunlight on the rose linoleum, in the middle of which she sat down, contorting her body so that as much of it as possible should feel the warm rays. From one of the houses opposite, a window-cleaner spied on her through a chink in the net curtains. Little thinking he could see her, she waved gaily. But the man made an amorous gesture, which sent her, with a plunge, into the bath.

" Another four hours," she thought, " and all must be ready. The cane chair between the two windows—two little chairs from the shop— three perhaps. The shop windows can be left unshuttered unless in the crush someone is likely to smash the plate-glass. A notice on the shop-door, though some malicious boy will probably deface it. A notice inside the shop window will be better. ' Closed till 3 P.M.'

65

Unless, of course, the shutters have to be put up. Four chairs. A rug for the more nimble ones, though I am the only one who will sit on it, I dare say. Hilary's room can be plundered. And, I must not forget, hot coffee, lemonade, whisky and soda, and plenty of gin. And the sandwiches still to make."

She soaped herself well, and, stretching a hand up to a glass shelf over the bath, poured a little scent, the present from a former admirer, into the water, and watched the cloudy rings curl round her sides. The patch of sunlight shifted, struck the edge of the bath, and gently crept along the water. Gloria lay back and sniffed the warm perfume, till the sun slid up the wall and touched the bottles on the shelf. Looking lazily upwards, she could see bright streaks of light through the greenish glass.

She got out of the bath, sprinkled a big towel with powder, another present from the same man, and dried herself till she was pink all over. Then, putting on her dressing-gown, she darted back to her bedroom, and began to dress, though she could not resist between each garment, running to the window and looking out. Thanks to the complete demolition of the opposite house, a large sweep of the Brompton Road could be seen. " Almost better than a direct view," she thought. " Indeed, the Lord is with me."

When she had finished dressing, she went out on to the balcony, the only second-floor balcony in Lithe Street, and looked down. From the Lloyd-Muce's balcony floated a big Union Jack, and two other flags whose names Gloria did not know. " I have forgotten about the flags," she confessed to herself, but felt happier when she remembered the red, white and blue Chinese umbrellas which her guests were to use. The effect would be more original, and no less loyal.

For the tenth time she paced the length of the balcony. It would only hold four chairs besides the big one. Another six inches, and perhaps a box or footstool could have been squeezed into a corner. Where the rug would go, she could not imagine. She would certainly have to sit on someone's toes—or knees. The congestion had its charm after all. It was lucky she had not

67

to entertain Mr. Lloyd-Muce, in his dozen over-coats. What a number of people in the street! Were they lining up already? The air was fresh and beautiful.

She went into her bedroom again, and heard Mr. Lace's shuffling footsteps passing the door. The thought of his gloomy face depressed her, but she hurried downstairs after him, and almost leapt on to his shoulders in the speed of her descent.

" Good morning, Gloria," he said. " What are you singing? "

She rushed past him into the room at the back of the shop, and turned on the electric kettle and egg-boiler which Lucima had already prepared.

" I'm singing ' Hail Festal Day,' " she answered.

" Is it appropriate? "

" You know what to-day is, Hilary, surely? "

" Yes. There won't be any buses and the crowd 'll be so thick that I can't get to the tube. And I've got to be at the office at a quarter-past ten."

" Will they want you to report for them, do you think ? "

" Oh dear, no. This affair isn't in my line. I'm all right when it's a case of saying ' Nothing was heard but the falling of a tear into the font,' but this caters for the camera pure and simple. No, it's about some other stuff."

" You'll be back though, won't you ? "

" Back for what ? "

" Have you forgotten ? To-day's the day of my party."

" Oh yes, so it is. Well, I hope you'll enjoy it."

" But you're coming, aren't you ? "

" Would you miss me if I didn't ? "

She turned away and cut some bread. His pathos was becoming unbearable. At first he had kept it for after dinner—later it appeared at tea-time. And now—before they had begun breakfast—it was excessively matutinal.

" There will," she said cruelly, " certainly be less of a squash if you don't come. But you needn't bother about that. I've made plans for all emergencies."

69

" Then you hoped I mightn't come ? "

" Don't argue with me. I'm too cheerful to be sympathetic. Here's your egg."

" Thank you."

" Bread, butter, salt, pepper."

She patted each of them demonstratively.

" Mr. Lloyd-Muce had a better night."

" How do you know ? "

" Lucima told me, when she brought my tea."

" Then he'll see it too."

" See what ? Really, Gloria, you are being a little absurd about this most ordinary event. It might be the founding of the new Jerusalem by the fuss you're making. And not content with watching it yourself, you have to give a party and badger other people into watching it too."

" At least," she said, less vivaciously, " it's the only time my balcony has been of any use at all. And with the house opposite only just pulled down, it would have been disgraceful to do nothing. Besides, I can't remember a procession in Brompton Road before."

"How many people are you expecting?" he asked, feeling that he had been too much of a wet blanket.

"Lady Hoobrake and her son."

"That's good. She's been a splendid customer. But why the son?"

"She asked if she could bring him. Besides I suspect that he introduced her to us really. I had a little talk with him once about the hat Miss Graham bought. That's two. Mr. Balcony and a friend of his who's staying with him, Captain Somebody. Oh, and Lady Hoobrake's brother, General Harrier, who's staying with her."

"Why Balcony? And who is he?"

"You know quite well who he is, or you wouldn't have asked that question second. You've met him in the shop."

"Why, then?"

"Because I like him."

"And why his friend?"

"Because he asked if he could bring him."

"Everybody in Lithe Street seems to have a visitor to bring."

71

" What does it matter ? There's room for you."

" You might have asked someone else."

" Whom ? "

" The Lewins or Joe Bamie."

" Oh, that crew. I couldn't face theatrical back-chat to-day."

" You've invited your customers. You might have asked someone who'd be useful to me. Joe Bamie's a very influential man."

He spoke, she thought, exactly as if they were husband and wife and had all things in common. It was quite time she took a stronger line about that partnership of theirs. If only his wretched capital hadn't been quite so useful! But he had seemed so biddable at first, and she supposed at one time she hadn't been quite sure that she would never come to care for him. Still, he had crept into her life insidiously—like a disease, to use one of his favourite metaphors. And without great ado, there was no being rid of him.

" Another egg, Hilary ? "

"Thank you. I'm not expecting any luncheon."

" I'm having sandwiches and whisky and soda for them."

" They won't all come starving, will they ? They're not so very far from their own larders, after all."

" It's a party."

He was about to prolong the unprofitable conversation with a retort, when Gloria rose and went upstairs, leaving him to a sour meditation. He ate his second egg, however, with relish, and when he left the house, resolved at all costs to be back in time for the procession.

Meanwhile Gloria was busy with a thousand small tasks, and Lucima, in the middle of a far less spirited employment, thought she had never seen so radiant a worker.

First the bed in Gloria's room was made into a settee, and strewn with bright cushions. The dressing-table became a sideboard. With the wardrobe nothing could be done. A few photographs and a large olive-wood box, the present of an admirer, were hidden and replaced by other photographs of more distinction but less interest.

Then Gloria went downstairs and made the sandwiches. Indeed she had to go up and down nearly twenty times, in the course of her arrangements. The throng in Brompton Road persuaded her to put up the shutters in front of the shop window, though it was a pity to lose the chance of attracting customers when the neighbourhood was so unusually populous. She did not trouble to affix a notice as to closing hours.

At a quarter-past eleven, having prepared everything but herself, she set about this final task, and was on the point of borrowing a new hat from the shop stock, when she decided not to wear a hat at all. She wore a thin creamy material, suggestive of ices eaten under chestnut trees, striped tents, the splash of waterfalls and the music of a distant roundabout.

She went with a book to the balcony and sat down in the big chair which Lady Hoobrake was afterwards to occupy. The sun was becoming powerful, but the house-side shielded her from it, and there was no need yet to use a patriotic parasol. A man with ices had stopped in front of the shop window, and a crowd had already taken up a position across the end of Lithe Street. A small motor-car came down the street, tried to pass and was sent back by a policeman. There were several policemen about and some of them were mounted. A first-aid post was established by the side of the demolished house. " We shall get the best of both worlds," Gloria thought.

She looked many times up Lithe Street to see if any of her visitors were approaching. She had given Lucima no instructions to admit them, and wished to see them before they arrived. The long street stretched somewhat tawdrily, half in sunlight, half in shadow. She strove to fix the point on the shadowy side where the doors of Nos. 36 and 38 were. Between her house and No. 36 there were sixteen houses, whose frontages averaged ten yards apiece. It does not take long to walk a hundred and sixty yards. Lady Hoobrake, however, would sail slowly along, like a ship in full rig, making for port, with Aubrey, a flag on a high mast, fluttering by her side. Mr. Balcony would take big leisurely strides. As for the two unknown visitors, the captain and General Harrier, she surmised that the one's gait would be brisk and the other's energetic but gouty.

It is when one is waiting for people that one sees most of one's surroundings. Gloria studied the street as if she had to describe it in an essay and were observing it for the first time. A man wheeled a barrow up to the florid red portico of No. 3, and using that as his base, made sallies into the crowd and tried to sell medallions of the royal family, rosettes and practical jokes that could be carried in the pocket.

Twenty-two minutes out of the thirty million, which she could fairly expect still to live, went by, and she did not grudge their going.

Her visitors who had met on their contiguous thresholds descended on her in a compact body.

She ran downstairs and let them in.

Mr. Balcony introduced his friend, a fine clean-shaven man with blue eyes, strongly coloured cheeks and a furtive look.

" Captain Buchanan."

" You've all met, I suppose," she said, " on the way."

" Mr. Balcony and I are neighbours," said Lady Hoobrake.

" I was expecting five," murmured Gloria, finding after a count that her guests numbered four. " Oh, of course, the General."

" My brother sends you his thanks and compliments, Miss Swing, but regrets exceedingly that he cannot join your party. We left him, I fear, somewhat indisposed."

Gloria guided them upstairs. When they saw her transformed bedroom, and the point of vantage from which they were to watch, they exclaimed with delight.

" Should we take up our positions now, do you think ? "

" We might as well. There is so much to watch in a crowd."

" Besides, the head of the procession should reach us in ten minutes."

" There are drinks here. I hope you will all help yourselves."

" Well, thank you," said Captain Buchanan, " I don't mind if I do."

He helped himself to a large whisky and soda, before taking a seat.

" And where will you sit, Miss Swing ? We seem to have taken all your chairs."

" Oh, this is my place. I'll float about."

She pointed to a footstool in the corner, and tripped about over their feet, offering cushions, cigarettes and the Chinese umbrellas.

In the distance there was the sound of martial music.

" Let Aubrey sit on the footstool, Miss Swing."

" No, no. I prefer it."

" The heat of that walk, short though it was ! " said Lady Hoobrake. " And we have had such a difficult time. But it is delightfully fresh and airy here. Do you feel the heat, Captain Buchanan ? "

" I do, ma'am," he said, raising his glass.

Aubrey ostentatiously pulled a sheet of paper ruled for music and a pencil from his pocket, and, after a moment's thought, wrote down one note.

" Aubrey," said his mother imperiously, " have the goodness to put that away. It is most ill-mannered."

" I am writing a violin sonata," he said, in answer to the interrogatory looks of the others, " but I find myself continually using the semibreve, a most unfashionable note nowadays."

" Can you wonder that he exasperates his uncle ? "

There was a rap on the bedroom door, and Mrs. O'Doyle came in, followed by Major O'Hoone.

" Juliana ! "

" We squeezed in, my dear. Your treasure of a servant girl let us in. Surely it was but half an hour ago that I said to the Major, ' Why, Major, why shouldn't we use Gloria's balcony for once, with such a fine show to be seen ? ' But I had no notion of all this company."

" I'm afraid we're rather crowded as it is."

" No matter, my love. Look on us as if we weren't here. We'll stand behind the windows, won't we, Major ? "

Mr. Balcony rose from his chair by Lady Hoobrake and offered it.

"Lord, no. The gentleman is too kind."

Mrs. O'Doyle sat down, and the Major with a click turned his walking-stick into a seat and settled by her side. Mr. Balcony stood erect behind Gloria's footstool.

Gloria introduced the new-comers. Perhaps, after all, their volubility would add to the day's charm.

There was a sound of cheering in the street.

Captain Buchanan bent ingratiatingly towards Lady Hoobrake and pointed to his empty glass.

"Just a small one?" he suggested.

With a nod and a thin little smile she assented, and he scrambled through the window, and came back with two full glasses.

"A set of drunkards we are, to be sure," said Mrs. O'Doyle, as the Major performed a like office for her and himself.

"Mr. Balcony?" said Gloria.

"Thank you. Let me help myself!"

He was followed by Aubrey, who left the

sonata on his seat, as if to prevent it from being taken.

" In trouble again ? " Mr. Balcony asked him, when they were by the buffet.

" A row with my uncle last night—a very vulgar scene. Almost killed him though."

" You shot and missed ? "

" He had a fit."

Lady Hoobrake, who had by now taken many a sip at her brandy, and felt much reanimated, noticed the manuscript on Aubrey's chair, and when he came back, charged him again to put it away.

" If my brother were here," she said, more to the company than to her son, " I tremble to think what would happen."

Then she described, with many contradictions and corrections from Aubrey, how on the previous evening, when her brother was outlining a new career for his nephew, Aubrey had suddenly played ten loud chords on the piano and gone upstairs. The General, after a monologue which drove Lady Hoobrake in a swoon to her sofa, seized a hunting-crop that had belonged to Aubrey's grandfather, and ran upstairs with foam on his lips. He found Aubrey having a bath, pulled him out and beat him. After this exertion, the General fell on the floor—" in a fit," said Aubrey—" no, not in a fit, but breathless and overcome "—" purple in the face, panting and swearing "—" no, but greatly overcome "—and lay there, while Aubrey heartlessly dried himself and dressed. The General, aided by his servant, whom Aubrey did not summon for a long time, went to bed. A doctor was sent for and reassured the household. Later there was some sort of a reconciliation.

" He said I took it like a sportsman," said Aubrey, " and gave me ten pounds."

" No wonder the lad wants a soft seat to-day," said the Major with a grin.

" Do you never lock the door when you have a bath ? " Mr. Balcony asked.

" I forgot, that time. Can you wonder, now that you've heard what a happy home I have, that—— ? "

While he was speaking a loud burst of cheering echoed in the street.

82

"They come! They come!" cried Mrs. O'Doyle.

It was the head of the procession—a troop of cavalry and a band. Infantry followed, then more horsemen with gun carriages, a band of pipers, more infantry striding to the beat of drums, arms swinging, flags flying.

"Oh, the brave show, the gay cavalcade," said Mrs. O'Doyle.

Gloria rose from her footstool. Mr. Balcony was in the corner behind her, and she felt the roughness of his serge piercing her thin dress. So powerful were her feelings as the procession took its proud and vigorous course before her, that it seemed to her as if in that moment the whole of life, freed at last from the pains of birth and the tortuous struggles of an obscure adolescence, were attaining a brief but full maturity, and displaying itself with waving of streamers and flaunting of plumes for a few perfect minutes in the sunlight, while she from above looked on serenely and applauded with a smile.

"It is life passing," murmured Mr. Balcony.

Then came the Royal carriage and the Royal bow. A clock struck noon. The climax was over.

More pageantry followed, but it was less splendid. The appearance of a phalanx of women in uniform was greeted with special cheering by the crowd.

" Absurd," said Lady Hoobrake, " aping the men like that. How wretched they look ! "

" To all unprejudiced observers, the cock is a finer animal than the hen," said Mr. Balcony.

" Come, come, sir," said the Major, " you should have left that remark for one of the ladies."

" They might be ducks," Lady Hoobrake continued, " they waddle so."

" Ducks, madam, ducks," said the Major, on the point of making a pun.

The men fetched drinks. Mrs. O'Doyle leant over the balcony.

" Why," she said, " that must be Mr. Lloyd-Muce watching too."

Gloria looked down and saw on the balcony below a muffled figure grasping the iron rail with both hands and gazing dejectedly into the street. His wife was by his side, eyes flashing, chin drawn back. Gloria waved, and Mrs. Lloyd-Muce replied firmly but without abandonment. " If he could fall over," thought Gloria, " it would be for the best."

" Who are they ? " asked Mr. Balcony, joining her.

" The Lloyd-Muces. He's very ill. The doctor says he ought to go for a sea voyage, but they can't afford it."

" He'd better join us," said Captain Buchanan.

" Are you going for one ? "

" Captain Buchanan is taking me for a trip on my yacht," said Mr. Balcony.

" Your yacht, Mr. Balcony ? "

" I have hired one."

" When do you go ? "

A host of cares suddenly assailed her. The sunlight waned. Innumerable to-morrows, in cheerless array, closed in upon her and demanded caution, restraint, endurance and many other laborious qualities.

" On May the third," said Captain Buchanan.

" Oh ! "

" Why, there's my maid," exclaimed Lady Hoobrake shrilly, pointing to a figure hurrying down the street.

" Can the best have happened ? " Aubrey muttered.

" Could the girl be let in ? I fear she has a message."

" I'll go down at once."

" I'll come with you."

Lady Hoobrake followed Gloria downstairs. Gloria let the maid in, and left her alone with her mistress. " I'm wasting my time," she thought, hearing their low tones. But as she went irresolutely upstairs, Lady Hoobrake overtook her.

" He's gone," she said, " got up and gone to the station. O God ! Another flight ? "

The Major met her at the threshold of Gloria's bedroom.

" No bad news, I trust, dear lady ? "

" My visitor has gone. Aubrey, your uncle has gone—up, dressed and gone."

" Another glass, ma'am ? " urged Captain Buchanan, offering her a strong mixture.

" After these stairs—thank you."

" No message left ? " asked Aubrey.

" None but that he felt quite well."

" A wretched message."

" No doubt," said Mr. Balcony, " the thought of meeting you again was more than he could bear."

" He seemed to find my presence humiliating."

" As distressing as your own prospects must be."

" You're rather a Job's comforter, sir," Aubrey said, adding by the last monosyllable a touch of respect to his words.

" I do not comfort."

They were all now assembled in the bedroom; for even Mrs. O'Doyle, having seen the arrest of a pick-pocket, and a fat man in a fit, found no more in the view to divert her.

" And now," said Mr. Balcony, " why should you not show us your wares ? "

" Yes, yes, a private view."

" I fear," said Gloria with a curtsy, " that I have little for you, gentlemen."

"Come, come," said Mr. Balcony, "we have our wives and sweethearts."

Gloria led the way downstairs. Captain Buchanan and the Major brought up the rear, thoughtfully carrying the drinks between them. Gloria turned on the light—for the shutters were still up—and made an improvised display.

"This," she said, "was recommended to me as a *dernier cri*, and this—though in style it is the opposite—as one also."

"If I were stout," said Lady Hoobrake, "I should choose that."

The Major winked.

"And that's the one for me," said Mrs. O'Doyle. "But, love, your prices are not for my purse."

"Two guineas."

"Let her have it," said Mr. Balcony. "Mrs. O'Doyle, the toque is yours."

A scene of great animation followed. Everybody talked at the same time. Aubrey, unasked, gave the imitation of a mannequin addressing herself first to the young wife of an old husband and then to the young husband of an old wife.

Mrs. O'Doyle pranced and Lady Hoobrake strutted. They all drank. Gloria felt as if she were a customer.

Mr. Balcony, in addition to buying a hat for Mrs. O'Doyle, bought one for Lady Hoobrake and one for Gloria, and when someone raked out a bronze straw helmet that might have been designed for Bellona herself, he suggested that the party should send it at his expense to Mrs. Lloyd-Muce. To this gift was added a thick woollen muffler for Mr. Lloyd-Muce. And not content with this munificence, he turned to Captain Buchanan and said, " Here ! Take this for your lady."

" A wife ? " cried Lady Hoobrake. " You are married ? "

" Yes, ma'am—in every port."

Meanwhile, Lady Hoobrake had bought six hats for herself, and Aubrey was bargaining over a purple tassel which he thought he could adjust to his dressing-gown. Gloria noted down eagerly the miraculous draught of orders, leaving her visitors to roam about and ransack the shop at their pleasure.

Mr. Balcony came up to her and said, " I have sent Captain Buchanan upstairs to make our present to the Lloyd-Muces."

" Now that we've played the fool,"—she said, thinking that he would admire a sudden return to sagacity.

" How will it help us, you mean, in a hundred years ? "

" Perhaps laughter vibrates for ever in silly little waves."

" It is the anticlimax," he said, " that I used not to be able to endure—taking down the flags, putting out the lights, going to bed. I have told Buchanan to ask the Lloyd-Muces to be my travelling companions."

" On the voyage ? "

" Please raise no prudent objections."

Past thoughts which she had had about him came fragmentarily into her mind—" distorted view . . . from a peculiar angle . . . works backwards, yet anticipates . . ."

" She will think you," she said, banishing those thoughts, " extravagant. She will refuse. Besides, Captain Buchanan is somewhat drunk."

" To that she will accustom herself. It does not impair all his faculties."

" Where are you going ? You have sprung this on us very suddenly. It shocks me."

" We are going to Africa—to Gahta."

" Oh ! "

" It is a little port, actually in foreign territory."

" How long will you be gone ? "

" The trip," he said with some gravity, " should take some four months. My yacht, though seaworthy and comfortable, is slow. Buchanan is under my orders."

" The Lloyd - Muces ——," she said, and thought of them without enthusiasm.

" Lady Hoobrake, I dare say, would join us."

" Yes, and her son, and Mrs. O'Doyle, and Major O'Hoone. Why not ask the whole party ? "

" An excellent suggestion. Let me count my cabins ! "

He pulled a piece of paper from his pocket, and studied it. Gloria watched him with apprehension. Had he no other friends, she wondered ? No relations ? And how many cabins would there be ? Then he went over to Lady Hoobrake and spoke to her in a soft voice. Gloria heard her say, " Well, I declare ! " twice, and went over to the door in order to hear more. But Captain Buchanan, swaying slightly, came in, followed by Mrs. Lloyd-Muce.

" The lady would like to see you, sir, in person."

" I have had, sir," said Mrs. Lloyd-Muce, holding herself erect with a virginal stiffness, " a most extraordinary proposal. May I ask if it has been made as a joke—a joke in vile taste ? "

" Madam," said Mr. Balcony, and drew her as if by magnetism to a distant corner of the room.

" O God," thought Gloria, " they'll all accept. They'll all accept."

" Now this tassel," said Aubrey.

" Oh, take the tassel. Have it for sixpence. Pay when you like."

He wrapped it up noisily in tissue paper and gave her an I.O.U.

" I had faith once that everything would be for the best," thought Gloria, " and could see in

all events a special omen for me. But now—
it is like searching for character-drawing in a
detective story, or reading between the lines of
a time table,—I cannot gild my disappointment.
Had he wanted me, he would have asked me
first. I am out of touch with life to have imagined
that it could be otherwise. Lady Hoobrake has
gathered that Mrs. Lloyd-Muce was a peer's
daughter. Mrs. Lloyd-Muce melts. I am a shop-
assistant, and my customers come to my shop to
see one another, and make their social engage-
ments in a most eighteenth-century way."

Mrs. Lloyd-Muce shot out a hand.

" I've had a life of surprises," she said loudly,
" but this is the biggest. Good-bye." And with
a nod to the company she went out.

Gloria's customers muttered together. She
felt detached from them.

" A glass," said the Major, " to our reunion
—and our host."

" To our hostess," replied Mr. Balcony with
a courtly gesture towards Gloria.

" Our host and hostess," they said and
drank.

"And who are they?" Gloria asked, as if the question were an alternative to a burst of tears.

"Miss Swing," said Mr. Balcony, "we shall all be charmed if you will come with us to Gahta."

She bowed and raised a glass to her lips.

Then the door opened and Mr. Lace shuffled in.

"I have one cabin left," said Mr. Balcony. "A small and rather uncomfortable one. But during the voyage we may have accommodation to spare."

He spoke like an optimistic hotel-manager, though nobody said so. While Gloria explained to Mr. Lace the offer which had been made to him and swept away his incredulity and caution with many a rap on the floor with her foot, the party began to disperse. Mrs. O'Doyle and the Major, realising that a free luncheon was not to be part of the entertainment, were the first to say good-bye. Then Lady Hoobrake felt the need of lying down, sent Aubrey outside to find a taxi, and when it became evident that he was having no success, or not trying, tottered up

Lithe Street on Captain Buchanan's arm. Mr. Balcony also took his leave.

" If you wanted me to come," said Gloria, " why did you ask me last, knowing me the best ? "

" For that reason," he said, and went out with a smile.

Mr. Lace now explained the cause of his lateness at the party and reiterated his disapproval of what he judged to have been the " goings-on " at it. " As for this madcap expedition," he said, " conceived in a moment of drunken folly — this acceptance of a lunatic hospitality. . . ."

" You'll do no good," Gloria interrupted, " as long as you model your articles on Dr. Johnson."

And cutting him short, she went upstairs to her bedroom, locked the door and shut her eyes.

In the almost empty street, a woman's voice was saying, " I don't hold with it, don't hold with it, never did, and never shall."

III

THE JOURNEY

(1)

GLORIA shut her eyes, and leant her head against the warm brown paint.

"I don't hold with it," a woman's voice was saying from the seat behind, "don't hold with it, and never shall. It's easy to lose your ideals. I might have lost my own. I might have been rich, I might have got back my health, I might even have had a child, but my sense of duty to Dick was too strong. 'Come with me,' Archie said many a time, 'just send a telegram and I'll fetch you and take you right away. Dick doesn't need you. I'll see he's provided for. What's keeping you back from me?' I hardly knew. Each time I wrote to him, using the dear little pink blotter he gave me, I wondered what it was. 'Duty,' I thought, 'duty.' But how did I come to have these notions of duty, I ask you? 'You are a wicked woman,' I told myself, 'and will go to Hell.' But it wasn't Hell that kept me back. Besides I could always have repented afterwards, and if I'd have been unlucky enough to have a sudden death, I believe that God would somehow have made allowances for it. After all, other people have done these things and managed to repent and be saved, and it would have been very unfair if I wasn't given a chance to get out the two words. No, it was more than religion that kept me straight. It was duty; deep down inside each of us duty lies, and it takes something to bring it up. So I stayed with Dick, though he grew more savage and ailing, and waited by him till he died. And all the while Archie sent me letters and telegrams from Rome, and Vienna, and Buda-Pest, and told me of his gay life. And the day Dick died I got a letter saying Archie had married a Hungarian actress. But by then I'd got a grip of my ideals and bore up as I've borne up ever since."

Gloria ceased to listen to the voice, and

heard instead the waves breaking on the supports of the pier, the distant band playing in the concert hall on the shore, an indistinct sound as of someone shouting through a megaphone a long way off, and the flapping of a sail or flag against a post. She was very tired. Packing, two unpleasant conversations with Mr. Lace, five interviews with his detestable sister who was to conduct the *Maison Swing*, forethought exercised over a hundred details, and alternations of very private hopes and forebodings, had used up her nervous energy.

As she fell asleep in the sheltered nook, it seemed to her as if she were lying on her back in a vast bed in a darkened room, though a bar of bright sunlight marked the chink of open window at the bottom of the dark green blind, and one could hear the sound of a mowing-machine purring on the lawn, and the wispy voices of children playing in the lower garden. And she enjoyed the day wearing itself out peacefully and aimlessly, the cool seclusion of her room, the physical pleasure of a calm dissolution. " The sense of duty," she thought—or rather dreamt she thought, because at the same moment an imaginary butterfly flitted from a dahlia to her cheek—" is, when calmly considered, the silliest of the senses." And for ten minutes she dreamt of silly people, sitting about in the courtyard of a madhouse, while the warders laughed and spat, and she from her bed laughed too and explained to someone who was not there why she felt no pity.

A hand pressed her shoulder. She looked up and saw Mr. Balcony.

" I've been asleep."

" Are you sorry to wake ? "

" I was having a satisfactory dream—knowing that what I wanted to be true was true."

" The Lloyd-Muces have arrived. Lady Hoobrake has lost one of her boxes. O'Hoone has had a row with a publican. We sail at seven."

" When do we embark ? "

" At any time. One takes a taxi to the harbour."

" I feel I should like ten days here."

" Only because you are going so soon."

They walked to the edge of the pier and looked

over. A fat man in a tight blue bathing-suit was sprawling on one of the girders and blowing his nose into the sea. A rowing-boat containing three women and two men passed, a hundred yards away. The women laughed hysterically every time one of the men pretended to drink out of an empty bottle. A purple and gold jelly-fish floated under the pier.

Mr. Balcony took some pennies from his pocket, and they made a tour of the automatic machines. His strength at the punch-ball returned the penny. Half a dozen children gathered round to watch. For another penny Gloria had her fortune told. " You are going a long journey," said the card, " but you will meet your love at a house with trees round it." A band under a striped canopy struck up a waltz.

They walked to the end of the pier and went through the turnstile on to the promenade. Six feet below them a multitude of children played with spades and buckets, while arch nursemaids sat gossiping on the sands and eating sweets out of twisted paper bags.

" Does it strike no chord ? " Gloria asked

Mr. Balcony, who had been silent for a few minutes.

" Each one of us," he answered, " has a beach somewhere to look back on, I suppose. I have one. On the last day of the first summer holiday that I can distinguish as such, a man dressed in black—or my imagination has since so dressed him—came up to me and said, ' Little boy, what will you be when you are thirty, forty, fifty? Of what disease will you die? How likely are you to live happily? Think it over. It's an important thought. Is it going to be worth while? ' He said much the same to other children also, but they put out their tongues at him, and emptied buckets of salt water over his patent-leather shoes. I wept behind a bathing-machine until a little girl came up and made advances to me."

" Did you respond? "

" I don't think so."

" Tell me some more about your early life."

" I have been trying to look upon it, as if it were a story, written by and about people whom

I shall never meet. Yours would interest both of us much more."

" I was brought up with every luxury."

" A clergyman's daughter ? "

" My father was a financier. He went bankrupt and died. My mother died when I was three. Her capital was tied up. I get the income of it."

" You cannot lay your hand on a lump sum."

" No. That is why I had to take a partner in my business."

" It is a key to innumerable lives. No goose, but little silver eggs half-yearly."

" Was that your position ? "

" No, not at all. I inherited some capital from an uncle, trebled it in wise investments, and have been living on it—on the capital, not the income —ever since."

" At least, the yacht seems prosperous."

" Hired, like a taxi."

" Still—a yacht."

They had reached the door of the hotel at which the party were spending the day.

" I shall go in," she said, " and sleep in an arm-chair in the conservatory."

" I shall walk up the hill."

" Which hill ? "

" That one," he said, and pointed to a long stretch of ground rising gently but continuously behind the hotel, and covered with houses and small gardens. On the topmost ridge was a severe stone house, on the roof of which, dominating the countless villas of the sprawling sunlit town, an immense notice displayed the words BOARDING-HOUSE to the distant naked eye. In line with this notice Mr. Balcony's sweeping forefinger paused.

" Why go there ? " she said. " But perhaps it's reasonable—a good contrast to this exotic trip of ours. Have you ever wondered why we are all coming with you ? "

" Each of you has two or three reasons. I know them all."

" I don't know yours—the reasons for which you invited us."

" I told you, I wanted no one whom I really knew."

" Do you think we shall regret coming ? "

" Most certainly you will—for a time."

" Supposing we deserted you at the gang-way ? "

" Could you ? ' This exotic trip of ours,' as you called it ? "

" Well, wait and see," she said, somewhat angered by the hall-boy, who had thrice made as if to open the door for her.

" I shall be back before six," said Mr. Balcony, raising his hat.

"*Au revoir*, then.   Be good."

She watched him passing a row of shrubs in painted green tubs, went inside and sat down in the conservatory.   Her head buzzed with per-plexing thoughts, but they were speculative rather than constructive.   Of the overwhelming emotions which she had promised herself, there was, as yet, no sign, and it was in vain that she gave a sensual twist to her meditation.   In the distance she heard Lady Hoobrake addressing an official.   Aubrey, she remembered, had gone to a cinema.   The little wretch—how would he manage in tropical parts ?   Mr. Lloyd-Muce was resting in a bedroom thoughtfully provided by

Mr. Balcony. (Had Mr. Balcony a kind heart?)
Mrs. O'Doyle and the Major would be watching
the pierrots, the coarsest of the pierrots. Mrs.
Lloyd-Muce was in the bedroom, making special
tea, no doubt with a collapsible spirit-lamp. With
her, no risk of fire. Why account for them all
like this—like a nursemaid in Kensington Gardens, who has parted with a red-coated soldier,
Boer - War period, and ticks off her charges
with greasy fingers? " Master Sammie getting
weighed, Miss Ursula by the kiosk with her 'oop,
Miss Bella and Master Jim in the pram—but
where's Master Leopold? Drat 'im! " And she
would pick up her long skirts (Boer-War period),
and run in the wrong direction. If only they
could all be lost, take to such vice as the town
afforded, perish in duels. For Mr. Lace, due at
six, a railway accident. They pricked, these
thorns in the flesh. Somehow the party would
lack the radiance which, in advertisements,
tempts the traveller. It was hard to picture them
sitting through the beauteous orient night,
turning ecstatic faces on one another and quaffing
champagne. Still, a few hours would show a

change. The philosopher debates the immortality of the soul and drinks hemlock. "Soon," he says, as a stiffness rises through his limbs, "soon I shall know what there is to be known." And his disciples discuss "knowledge" and whether the word was aptly used in such a context.

At all events, there would be long hours when, sitting on deck, one could read part of all that one had neglected in English literature. One would come back and take one's place amongst those who talked of such things. "Fielding? Ah, yes, but you try Tobias Smollett." One would come back changed, improved. But who had called for Smollett and the like, except Hilary's friends, peering at her during *entr'actes* with intellectual faces? "Tchehov? Pirandello? *Vieux jeu.* Shaw." Who was *Vieux jeu*, she had once asked; but the fault had lain in a vile pronunciation, not in her. "The famous Pomeranian," Joe Bamie had tittered, while Hilary blushed. Pale intellectual faces. It was a good thing for Hilary to see men like Mr. Balcony and the Major and Captain Buchanan.

Even the Major and Captain Buchanan were better than Joe Bamie and Hilary.

At all events, one would come back changed, if not improved. " This exotic trip of ours "— detestable phrase, bright, fluffy, winter-sports-girlish—could not fail to leave a mark. Twice already that year she had felt a change beginning, on St. Valentine's day — " a delusive day of early spring," as a melancholy journalist might have described it—and on the day of the procession. And now, waiting in the conservatory, watching through half-shut eyes the flies crawling on the laths of the badly lowered venetian blinds, she was wondering about the change again. Perhaps she ought to have insisted that it was no use to her, either, coming with people she knew so well—Hilary, Mrs. O'Doyle. Even the Major recalled the slightly loose gentility to which she had deliberately adapted herself. " I might have been a *family-girl*," she thought, " with a protruding chin." *Familjeflicka* : she laughed silently at the old joke. " And in the matter of the fisheries, Norway is a difficult *concurrent*." She told herself the whole story.

It was one of those detached episodes, which make an agreeable memory and suggest no moral responsibility or neglected duty.

Lady Hoobrake came into the conservatory and peered round short-sightedly. Gloria watched her, as she watched the flies, hoping not to be recognised.

" The least you can do," Lady Hoobrake said to Aubrey, who was evidently there, though Gloria could not see him, " is to learn to swim during the trip."

(" This exotic trip of ours.")

" Will there be a swimming-bath ? "

" And I shall speak to Mr. Balcony about your Spanish. Four hours a day, mind. I can't abide these wicker chairs."

" Then you'll have to go back to the drawing-room."

" It smells."

They went back however, and Gloria, wondering why she was so sleepy, feel asleep, and dreamt that she was lying in a vast bed in a darkened room, though a bar of bright sunlight marked the chink of open window at the bottom

of a dark green blind, and one could hear the
hooting of a steamer leaving port and almost
see the thin line of foam that stretched behind it,
as it became a speck on the horizon. Then a
loud voice said, " Never use a word of three
letters where one of two will do," and she awoke
to see Major O'Hoone and Mrs. O'Doyle looking down at her, as if her sleep had been inelegant.
" My face is probably red," she thought, " not
to say blotchy."

" I dreamt," she said, giving a point to her
dream which it had not possessed, " that you
had gone without me."

They were both drinking brandy and soda.

" Is it six ? " she asked.

" Yes rather," the Major answered. " Want
any help with your kit ? "

" He's as breezy as the sea itself," said Mrs.
O'Doyle proudly.

Gloria yawned and rose.

" Just five minutes, and I'll be ready. Has
Mr. Lace come ? "

" He's tinkering with his trunk on the steps.
The cord broke."

Of course Hilary tied his luggage up with string.

" Then he'll need your help more than I do."

The Major emptied his glass.

" I'm afraid all my energy's for the fair sex, this afternoon. I'm not given to trapesing after my own ! "

" Well, I dare say I shall need you later on."

" Words of three letters ! Words of one letter for him," she thought, as she went to the ladies' cloak-room.

When she had made herself ready, she found three taxis by the hotel entrance. Mr. Balcony had gone to the boat, and left word for them to follow. His servant would be at the harbour and guide them on board. He had paid the hotel bill—luncheon for six, tea for three with one extra portion of milk, the double bedroom in which the Lloyd-Muces had taken sanctuary.

Gloria got into the first taxi with the Major, Mrs. O'Doyle and Mr. Lace, who was wearing a very thick overcoat and a nautical cap. He greeted Gloria as if they had not met for six

months, and complained of the dust in his throat.
Lady Hoobrake, lacking one box, but still
possessing many, followed with Aubrey in the
second taxi and the Lloyd-Muces had the
third.

In a procession they drove along the promenade, past the winter-gardens, through a tortuous
street up hill into the old town, then down hill
again to the harbour. They got out on the
quay and were saluted by N'Gambi who caused
an official to allow them to pass through a barrier.
Their luggage was collected, disappeared and
reappeared on the deck of a small launch. At
the mouth of the harbour, white with pale green
awnings, half in the sunlight, half in shadow, lay
Mr. Balcony's yacht, the *Percy*.

The sight of it brought most of them a
thrill.

Then they stepped on to the launch, clumsily,
as if making an experiment. Mr. Lloyd-Muce
sat down. The others stood and turned their
heads alternately towards the yacht and the
shore. A shrill whistle blew and there was
a churning of waters. The breeze seemed

suddenly to gather strength. Water appeared
between the launch and the jetty. There was a
smell as of fish secreted amongst tarred ropes.
Eyes scanned the distant waves. The nose of
the launch circled round in the direction of the
yacht. The quay, with its sheds, enclosures,
bales of merchandise and moored vessels, receded.

The Major said " Off we go," and hummed a
lively air. Gloria saw Mr. Balcony standing on
the deck of the yacht, with Captain Buchanan.
With more churning the launch swung into
position beside its objective. There were incomprehensible shouts. A gangway was let down.
" Unlucky to go first," whispered Mrs. O'Doyle.
But the caution was not needed ; for Mr. Lloyd-
Muce was with a mysterious unanimity helped
on board before the others. His wife followed,
then Lady Hoobrake, then Gloria. A blue arm
assisted her at the bottom, and another blue
arm at the top. She took both, though they
were unnecessary. Mrs. O'Doyle came next,
then the Major, then Aubrey and last of all
Mr. Lace who fell on all fours.

" The sign of a wedding," said Mrs. O'Doyle.

" And now," said Mr. Balcony, greeting them when they were all assembled, " let me show you your cabins."

They followed him into a dark and narrow passage, and the clock of the old church beside the quay struck the quarter before seven.

(II)

By turns the voyagers unpacked and went on deck to watch the sea, and when they found the sea monotonous, the land. They were passing the watering-places of southern England, and vied with one another in recollecting that the bay, harbour or Grand Hotel of such and such a town had such and such a shape. Dinner was at eight o'clock.

" Are we supposed to dress ? " asked Mr. Lace provocatively.

" Most gentlemen do," said the Major.

" Do exactly as you wish," said Mr. Balcony.

They all dressed, except Mr. Lloyd-Muce, who sat wrapped in rugs outside the door of his cabin and ate something in a bowl. Mr. Balcony provided champagne. The Major and Captain Buchanan drank many healths. Then everyone went out on deck again to watch the sea, the stars and blurs of light on the coast. A wind was rising, and the yacht began to sway.

"Do you want anything to read?" Mr. Lace asked Gloria, when bedtime had been agreed upon. "I have quite a library with me." She followed him into his cabin and he showed her, amongst other things, a set of Shakespeare in a miniature bookcase, each play forming a tiny volume.

"I will take this," she said, choosing *Pericles*. "I didn't know Shakespeare had written a play of this name."

"It isn't very—good reading," he said, and pressed *Henry the Fifth* upon her.

She took it, to avoid an argument, and went to her cabin, where in order to accustom herself to the novel gymnastic, she undressed, dressed and undressed again. During the night she heard many noises, pulling of ropes, clattering of cans, steps on the deck and once, when she was almost asleep, snatches of drunken song.

The next morning, when the stewardess, a gaunt woman, brought Gloria a cup of tea, the sun was jeering at her between bundles of grey cloud. By breakfast-time it was raining. During a fine interval a game of deck quoits was proposed, but most of the players found that the stooping had disagreeable consequences. During luncheon Mr. Lace left the saloon hurriedly, and was soon followed by Lady Hoobrake and Aubrey.

Only two out of the nine passengers came down to dinner—Mr. Balcony and Mrs. Lloyd-Muce. After a salmon mayonnaise, she broke the silence.

" They're a squeamish lot."

" Give them a few days," said Mr. Balcony.

" I've been to India and back four times, and was never sick once."

" Is Mr. Lloyd-Muce bearing up ? "

" Perfectly, thank you."

They said little else during the meal, but when their coffee was served in the lounge, Mrs. Lloyd-Muce, with a forward thrust of her face, said suddenly, " What's your game, Mr. Balcony ? "

" Whatever it is," he said, " it suits your purpose."

" Supposing," she said, " I make the others inquisitive ? Hadn't you better tell me ? "

" Supposing I enjoy their inquisitiveness ? "

" I shall watch you."

Captain Buchanan walked past them with a salute, and went into the saloon.

" That man's a drunkard, Mr. Balcony."

" There's no danger."

" And the other officers ? "

" All under my thumb."

" Where's the doctor ? You said there would be a doctor."

" Cabin No. 5.   He's ill."

" Pshaw ! "

" Oh, not sea-sick. Will you come and see him ? "

" Yes."

He led her to the doctor's cabin, and without knocking opened the door. A figure dressed only in a shirt was lying on a bunk at the far end, the face turned to the wall. An eider-down had slipped on to the floor.

Mr. Balcony picked it up and spread it over the bed.

" What's the matter with him ? "

" Let him be. He has a poor bedside manner, but he'll be ready for anything you want. I understand the business too."

" You ! "

" You can test me with questions, if you like."

" Are you qualified ? "

" No. But does that matter ? I gave you references, didn't I ? "

They left the doctor's cabin and walked round the deck. Mr. Lloyd-Muce sat in his chair outside his cabin, and nodded when they passed. It was the habit of Mr. Balcony's guests, subsequently, whenever they went by that part of the deck, to quicken their paces and look out to sea.

" What lighthouse is that ? " Mrs. Lloyd-Muce asked, when they reached the prow.

" Ushant."

" Oh ! "

" There's no shore within hail."

She laughed suddenly, and said, " I'm afraid

you think I'm a joyless creature. It's a pity the merry-makers are all in bed."

"Perhaps we shall have enough of them, later."

She said good-night, and went to put her husband to bed, while Mr. Balcony for nearly two hours contemplated the monotonous grandeur of the ocean.

(III)

Off the coast of Portugal the invalids began to creep on deck, and in another two days entered upon what was to be for a while their normal life. In the middle of the day they basked in the sun—at first imprudently; for many a complexion became suddenly blotched and blistered. At meals they talked loudly and quickly, ate too much food and masticated it insufficiently. Captain Buchanan and the Major organised games, competitions, charades and dances. Mr. Lace kept a serio-comic journal, somewhat in the style of Thackeray. He also wrote part of his old novel and began a new one. Gloria assured herself of her exhilaration. Mrs.

Lloyd-Muce spent most of her time with her husband, and hardly spoke to the others except at meals. Lady Hoobrake supervised her son's study of a Spanish grammar, and reminded him how good a post in Valparaiso awaited him, once he had mastered that tongue. To the others she was distantly agreeable, though she would from time to time suddenly pick out one of the party as a recipient of confidences, which her manner would seem later to withdraw. Aubrey endeared himself to few, though Mrs. O'Doyle made much of him. The doctor, tall, thin and sallow, appeared and disappeared like a ghost. When one spoke to him, he would give vent to a flood of technicalities and walk away. Mr. Lloyd-Muce, who during the rough weather had seemed to be regaining health, was suddenly seized with such grave symptoms that his wife was compelled to ask the doctor to visit him. It was whispered that the report was very sinister. But Mrs. Lloyd-Muce, her chin thrust out beneath the brim of her Bellona hat, sought for no sympathy. Mr. Balcony was as a professional amongst amateurs. He had an agreeable word for all. It was admitted that he was kind and generous, but the Major, when speaking of him, would sometimes wink and tap his head, and Mrs. O'Doyle would suggest a disappointment. No one, however, dared to behave disrespectfully in Mr. Balcony's presence, and the doctor, Captain Buchanan and the other officers obeyed him as if they were notes on a piano played by a skilful hand.

From time to time the *Percy* put into port to get supplies, but none of the guests went ashore. When Mrs. O'Doyle suggested an expedition at Gibraltar, Mr. Balcony told her that they were to remain there for half an hour only. As she said afterwards, "I dare say, if I'd wheedled him a bit, he'd have stayed long enough for us to go, only I was afraid that a whim might start him off again before we got back. And then, I ask you, where should we have been?" "At Gibraltar, I suppose," Aubrey replied to this rhetorical question, and eluded her when she made as if to box his ears.

This restriction to the boat was a disappointment to Gloria, who felt that the sea had small variety as compared with the land.

" I confess," she said wistfully to Mr. Balcony one evening, " I should like to go ashore. You see, I've never travelled."

" On the journey home," he said, " you shall see as much as you wish."

" Are we in a hurry then ? " she said.

" Every day is accounted for."

" Why ? "

" Because—having committed myself to nothing—I can't stop for anything."

He laughed with her at the openness of his evasion, and then seeing that she still seemed dispirited, gave her a few sheets of paper and told her to read them, if she wished, when she went to bed.

" But," he said, " you must ask me no questions. There are flaws in the marble, and I can't bother with them now. It's myself really I'm trying to mystify—not you."

She went at once to her cabin, undressed and read the papers in bed.

The manuscript was in pencil, and headed " Outline for Ch. 9 to 12."

" Attention," it began, " to my teeth, hands, feet and hair. Saw myself as I should be at 50 with a scholar's stoop, anæmic face, puffy eyes and bald pate—one whom conversationalists, except benign old ladies with nothing better to do—would ignore. A shout, perhaps, once a day from the other end of the room, ' Hi, Balcony, you know Greek. What was the Minotaur ? ' or, over the barrier of a newspaper, ' What does *isobar* mean ? '

" For a long time I asked myself if I was not merely vain.

" Exercises, morning and evening. (Factitious ideal, to break a poker with one hand.) Moustache, military air. Four years in the army —doing violence to myself rather than have others do it to me. External transformation. An oddity, but not negligible.

" Idle arguments with metaphysicians—their reluctance to consider pain, their insistence on duty and law. The mysticism with which I parried them. If reality exists, in their sense, is it impossible to apprehend it ? Perhaps in a work of art, the idea behind the visible, or the audible ? Once in touch, would one not cease to be bothered with nuisances, such as waiting for trains, or sympathy for others ? Find one's place in the harmony, if there is one. The more my actions seemed capricious, the more they would be ordained by the essential : hence, if you like, the more they would be free. Though who should I be, then, to care about freedom ?

" My adoption of inconsistent methods. Indifference to pain, indifference to pleasure. But which, in my life as nature intended it to be, was likely to predominate ? (I was hypnotised by that phrase ' as Nature intended me to be,' and resolved at all costs to be unnatural. Query : this subject already examined ?) Seeing myself altering. Since I now wish to be changed, when I am completely changed, I shall cease to wish to be changed.

" The process.

" Doubts and imperfections. The clinging to old ties. Joys of uprooting myself, joys nevertheless of memory. *Non sum qualis eram*. But the luxuries of this introspection are hazardous, even if I try simply to see myself as others see me. I look upon others as mirrors. They see me, robust and poker-bending; whisper 'well-preserved.'

"New friends for old. Alter my scenery. Why scenery, why friends? Form no new ties, but go slow. Dangerous to give up vices too abruptly. In the end, clear out. Make a machine and jump into it. A few hours' wringing of hands won't matter after a few hours. Does it matter to-day, that I had a pain yesterday when I burnt my fingers? Yes. (1) Because it leaves a nasty mark. (2) Because I dread the fire, and my style is cramped, not broadened. Note this rough and ready rule: *A thing cannot matter unless it matters to somebody.*

"Hence, by an agreeable transition, nothing matters (I can say, looking the universe in the face), unless it matters to me. And with this supreme confession——"

Here the manuscript came to an end. A few words were torn off the bottom of the last sheet.

Gloria beat the crushed pillows into shape, and relaxed her posture. "If I were more stupid," she thought, "I should say it contained many beautiful thoughts. If I were cleverer, I should understand it. Good night, everybody."

When she was almost asleep, she heard voices, one of them a woman's voice, outside her window, and caught the words "At once, please. Be quick! . . . Are you sure? I shall never forgive you, if it doesn't."

The next morning, Mr. Lloyd - Muce no longer sat in his accustomed place. But polite inquiries had little reward.

Meanwhile, it grew hotter every day. The passengers lay about under awnings, tongue-tied and sullen with their eyes staring angrily at the electric fans. From time to time thunderstorms swept down upon the boat, but gave small relief. Mr. Lace laid his work aside, and brooded over apprehensions which later he was to impart to others.

Lady Hoobrake drank and fainted—and drank again. When Mrs. O'Doyle and the Major could open their lips it was to complain. Gloria was oppressed with a melancholy lassitude which seemed timeless.

Aubrey barely left the bathroom except when driven out of it. Alone of the women, Mrs. Lloyd-Muce, her face the colour of her Bellona hat, made no change in her bearing or attire. And Mr. Balcony, alone of the men who were not sailors, went about unperturbed.

(IV)

An unexpected breeze and the scampering of feet drove Mr. Lace to his window. Looking out on to the deck, he saw a number of beings arrayed as Sirens, sea-monsters, dolphins and Tritons. His heart sank. It was evident that on board the *Percy* the deplorable customs, attendant upon " crossing the line," were not in abeyance.

It was after breakfast that the carnival took shape and harried the defenceless. A liberty was taken with each of the ladies (except Lady Hoo-brake, who was unaccountably still asleep), an

indignity practised on each of the men. Mr.
Lace's omission to shave was made good in
public. He contorted his lips into a frigid smile
which did not hide his resentment. The Major
had been to tropical parts before, and escaped
lightly. Aubrey, wearing spotless white, had
prepared himself for the ceremony, and surprised Mr. Lace and the Major by the effrontery
with which he advanced at Neptune's summons.
His jauntiness, however, changed to dismay when
he found that it was proposed to cut his hair, the
length of which he would exhibit by brushing it
forward over his face and biting it. No one paid
the slightest heed to his protests, and while his
head was being put in position, he contrived to
escape from his captors and darted towards his
cabin. The crew, who seemed to have licence to
misconduct themselves, pursued, and, after a
chase, caught him again. He was in tears.
"For God's sake," he screamed, "stop them,
Mr. Balcony."

Mr. Balcony sauntered up to Neptune, and
said something to the god which the others did
not hear.

"Now, young gentleman," said Neptune, "you can choose which you'll give up. Your 'air, or your two side teeth, which stick out like a rabbit's, and spoil your beauty. If you say your teeth, you can keep your 'air; if you say your 'air, you can keep your teeth. But one or the other it's got to be and will be."

Argument followed, and the ultimatum was pressed.

"Say before I count ten, or it'll be both—and your 'air first."

"Eight. Nine."

A pair of huge scissors almost closed over a handful of tresses.

"Teeth."

"No gas, mind, no cocaine, no freezing-mixture. Better say 'air."

"Teeth, damn you."

"Now don't you be saucy. This gentleman 'll do it for you very kindly."

This gentleman was Mr. Balcony, who took a pair of forceps from a case and beckoned. With white face Aubrey followed him to a seat at the end of the boat.

" Sit down.   Open your mouth."

A Siren brought a glass of water and a mouth-wash.

Then Mr. Balcony pulled out first one of the projecting teeth, and then, after a short pause, the other.   During the operations Aubrey made no sound, and hardly flinched.

" Good dog," said Mr. Balcony.

A cheer broke out, and Aubrey, enraptured with his own heroism, went up to Neptune, presented him with two small and glittering teeth, and drank his health in champagne.

Gloria felt ill and went to her cabin, while Lady Hoobrake, waking drowsily, found that her wrist-watch marked eleven.

(v)

Lady Hoobrake had had many excellent reasons for accepting Mr. Balcony's invitation. It was, in the first place, a free holiday, and she was able to let the house in Lithe Street on excellent terms to some Americans.   The company, to be sure, was mixed, but it included

Mrs. Lloyd-Muce, who was a peer's daughter, and Gloria, whose mother had shared with five sisters an obscure place in Debrett under the heading of "issue." On any other holiday Aubrey would have been uncontrollable, while he could never have a better opportunity for learning Spanish than on the boat. There was enough to eat and drink. Bills could not reach her. She was treated with courtesy by all, and especially by Captain Buchanan.

Mr. Lace, on the other hand, had only one reason for taking the voyage, and that reason was a source of bitterness. He had no regard for any of his fellow-travellers except Gloria. The sea distressed him, and he hankered for Fleet Street. After trying in vain to adapt himself, and to win success as a "life and soul," he grew morose, kept himself apart, and when addressed showed truculently that he wished for the charity of no one's friendship. When the need to speak possessed him, he uttered opinions which he knew would be unpopular, praised the ascetic life, denounced luxury, aped the professional moralist. The lounge and smoking-room he littered with

Fabian essays which he had packed by accident. He deplored the fact that the *Percy's* little library contained no book on the function of the individual in society, and began to write a monograph on that subject. One day he overheard Mr. Balcony saying to someone, " He reminded me of those elderly young men whom you might see in a vegetarian restaurant, badly dressed, short‑sighted and half‑bald, bending over a revolutionary pamphlet." Mr. Lace immediately took the remark to apply to himself, though in fact it had reference to a well-known actor, and from that moment so abhorred his host, that he almost felt affection for his fellow-guests.

To justify this abhorrence, and give it colour, he persuaded himself that Mr. Balcony was his rival in Gloria's regard.· It is indeed surprising that he had not realised before that it was so. When once, however, he had invented this truth in his imagination, he was quick to find evidences of it in reality, and to entertain of Mr. Balcony the most diverse and improbable suspicions.

The whole object of the expedition seemed to him suddenly sinister and nefarious. He loitered and listened in corridors, envisaged murders and sadistic orgies. The thought that he and Gloria were in the power of a madman became an obsession. He took each of the guests in turn for an accomplice, breathed dark hints, parried imagined plot with counter-plot. It was as if the sun had gone to his head.

One evening, after dinner, he saw through the open cabin-door Gloria sitting on her bed and mending a tear in a white silk pyjama-jacket. He suspected the garment, for no reason, of being Mr. Balcony's, and at the sight of it tip-toed into the cabin and shut the door behind him. Gloria raised her eyes in astonishment and displeasure. It was hot and thundery, and Mr. Lace was filled with an unwonted vitality. "After all," he thought, as he sat down on a small chair, "we only live once. Live dangerously! Live dangerously!"

"What do you want?" she said, when he had been silent for two minutes.

He paused for a beginning. Countless explanations, theories of life, revelations of himself and his passion, epitomes of human suffering, expressions of the ideal, flooded his mind with a luminous intensity. A dozen orations sprang to his lips, a dozen gestures convulsed his hands and feet. "Superman," he murmured to himself, "calm and cool. Strong, strong. Live dangerously. Think, speak, act, fearlessly, shamelessly."

"Why are you twitching like that?" she asked. "What do you want?"

It was his moment. He got up slowly, straightened himself, poised his head as if to deliver a tirade, and then, uttering the single word "You," jumped to the bed and flung himself upon her.

They skirmished for three seconds, and then the needle with which she had been sewing ran into his cheek. With a loud cry he slid on to the floor and lay there. Mr. Balcony's urbane face appeared at the little window. Gloria drew herself up with Amazonian dignity.

"Mr. Lace has assaulted me," she said, "but I have dealt with him."

"Indeed," said Mr. Balcony. "Well, they say that no ship is a ship without a seduction."

And he smiled and passed on.

With the feelings of one who has just dropped and broken a beautiful vase, Gloria surveyed the body on the floor—though, for her, no precious fragments lay there.

" Get up ! "

He sat, and pressed a handkerchief to his cheek.

" Have you any antiseptic ? " he asked huskily.

" I have some powder."

" No Pond's Extract ? "

" No."

" Was your needle sterilised ? "

" Of course not."

" Then," he said, " I shall probably get blood-poisoning or tetanus.   Let me look at it."

She searched the crumpled bed-clothes and the pyjamas which she had been mending, found the needle and gave it to him. He looked at it anxiously.

" Is that rust ? "

" Where ? "

" There, a quarter of an inch from the point."

" I can't see."

" Come to the light."

She got down from the bed and went with him to the window.

" I don't think so."

" I think it is."

" Well, what then ? "

" I shall probably get blood - poisoning or tetanus. That's all."

" Rubbish. Go to the doctor for something, if you're so frightened."

He hesitated, seemed about to say something and went out.

Gloria sat on the bed again, and powdered her face. " Fool," she thought, " interfering, meddlesome fool ! How typical of Hilary that his blundering brings me this misery ! ' They say that no ship is a ship without a seduction.' Cruel, selfish, indifferent. I am a fool not to have seen it before. Well, I know now. I'll waste no more thought upon him. I hate him."

She glowed almost with pleasure. This hatred was a real thing and brought its object into close touch with her. Its sharpness gave relief from mooning melancholy, its quick rise cut short lingering regrets. It was a proof of the genuineness of her feeling, and the past on which (she realised at the same time as she brushed the thought aside) she might for many a year still have to feed.

" But the present," she thought, " is full of torments. And there is this exotic trip of ours —still not half done—with its daily meetings, and the need for a face of brass and words to disguise thoughts, a new voice in which to lie."

As if there had been comfort in this last reflection, when Mr. Lace, after knocking at the door, came in again, she answered him in deeper tones than usual and gave a slightly American sound to her vowels. It was as though (adopting a small part of Mr. Balcony's scheme for self-regeneration) she had in some measure altered herself with her voice, and, as a stranger, found speech less of an effort.

" I couldn't find the doctor," he said quietly. " I knocked at his cabin but got no answer.

But Mrs. Lloyd-Muce had some stuff, and thinks I'll be all right now."

" I'm sorry I hurt you," she said. " It was by accident."

" I want you to forgive me if you can."

" No ship is a ship without a seduction."

" I'm very serious, Gloria."

" I am not affected by it. I am the same—towards you."

Her voice was very husky and deliberate as she said these words.

" I've been upset lately," he went on.

" What's the trouble ? "

" I don't know. I'm frightened of this trip."

" Why ? "

" I think Balcony's mad. I think—please don't laugh at me—I think he means to kill us."

" It sounds rather absurd, Hilary."

" He isn't sane or normal."

She said nothing.

" Were those his pyjamas you were mending ? " he asked suddenly.

" No. My own."

" I didn't know you wore pyjamas."

" I didn't know Mr. Balcony did."

" If you won't be serious with me——"

She looked fixedly at the floor, and Mr. Lace, having waited in vain for her to speak, walked out miserably.

(VI)

The doctor was speaking, and Mr. Lace, as if fearful of hearing his own death-warrant, listened by the door of the smoking-room, which was ajar.

" Last night," the doctor said, " I forged the last link in my theory. I told you of the almost harmless microbe I discovered in the tissues of the skin. This same microbe, though in its primary form it does small damage, when it has passed through a series of bodies with certain favourable characteristics, completely changes its nature. It develops a power to form spores, like the *anthrax bacillus*, and these spores can lie dormant for a period almost as long as that of my own observations. After the dormant stage, however, the microbe changes again, and appears this time in a form almost indistinguishable from that of the *spirachaeta pallida* or the germs of certain tropical diseases. It now quits the surface of the body and attacks the central nervous system, becomes pathogenic in the highest degree and defies all the remedies which we have at present for combating the ravages of microbes whose nature would seem to be similar. It remains in the organism which it has attacked till the death of that organism approaches, and then—here is the miracle— makes its way to the surface of the skin once more, and resumes its original and comparatively innocuous form."

" And then ? " Mr. Lace heard Gloria asking.

" And then the whole circle may begin again. Or, as I suspect, it may proceed differently. The truth is simply this. The substance of all microbes is the same, and it only depends upon environment what form this substance is to take. I hope, in a short while, to turn the *lactic bacillus* into the germ of tetanus, at will. Good night. I must go to my patient."

With quick jerking steps he passed through

the door behind which Mr. Lace was hiding, and went to his cabin. Mr. Lace went into the smoking-room by another door, and found Gloria sitting in a chair with her eyes shut.

" Hello ! " he said. " What are you doing ? "

" Resting."

" This trip," said Mr. Lace, " will be the death of us. When I think of your high spirits at the start——"

" Don't. Don't."

" Mr. Lloyd-Muce is much worse."

" How do you know ? "

" I heard the doctor talking to Mr. Balcony."

" What did he say ? "

" Who ? "

" Mr. Balcony."

" He said that the hospital at Gahta was always full of Johnson's fever, and there were few worse deaths to die."

There was a pause, broken by a shrill cry of laughter from the deck where Mrs. O'Doyle was dancing alone.

" We're going mad," said Mr. Lace. " This is a nightmare."

" You've lost your nerve."

" We must get away—escape."

" We shall land in a few days. Besides, how ? "

" We could bribe some of the men to put us off in a boat."

" In mid-ocean ? "

" It isn't *mid* now," he said, without being amused.

" What a crew we should be."

" Tell me, Gloria, are you enjoying yourself ? "

She burst into tears and motioned him to go away.

(VII)

It was nine o'clock on a calm and clear night. From the saloon came the tinkle of the piano on which Lady Hoobrake was practising a song for Major O'Hoone. One member of the crew was playing a concertina, another a mandoline and another a child's dulcimer. Captain Buchanan, inside his cabin, was singing in a thick muffled voice :

" Give me the East with its parrots and wines,
  Parrots and wines, parrots and wines,
Give me the East with its concubines,
  Its dancing-girls and concubines."

The sounds were mingled by a little scented breeze, and sounded like a gay piece of chamber music written by a modern composer.

Mr. Balcony met Gloria, whom the breeze had roused somewhat from her lethargy, walking round the deck.

" Tell me," he said, " what is the matter with Mr. Lace ? "

" He is wretched for three reasons," she said. " He thinks that you intend to scuttle the ship with us all aboard, he fears tetanus from a scratch on the face, and he is love-sick for me."

" You scratched him ? "

" Unwittingly, with a needle."

" Love-sick, he clings to life ? "

" As the drowning."

" When I loved, I took chloroform, was sick and loved no more.   What is his life that he should treasure it ? "

" It is his."

" What has it given him ? What noble action has he done, what exalted thought has he experienced, what passionate memory stored up ? "

" None."

" How then could he bear a slow death ? "

" As people do. When they cannot bear it, they die."

" But I suppose it is hardly reasonable to wish to live in order that one may prepare oneself for dying ? It is a theological notion, which as a nineteenth-century freethinker he must abominate."

" Let us talk of someone else."

They said nothing for a while, but the ship's music droned on, and was amplified suddenly by the beautiful voice of a sailor singing :

"Ah ! bear in mind, this garden was enchanted."

The air, thought Gloria, was full of the scent of cloves and cedar-wood, and warm wax.

" It is," said Mr. Balcony, " because your life is bound to Lithe Street and the idylls of South Kensington, that you are here like a ghost of yourself. The body has been stolen from the soul, which flutters whining past the Knightsbridge tube. 'When,' you will say afterwards, drawing velvet curtains at a November dusk, 'when I was in Africa, we ate beans and rye with a sauce of crocodile's marrow,' as we say 'I have been to John o' Groats, you know,' hoping that no one will ask what business took us there."

"I still hope," she answered, "for some experience——"

"An experience to carry back to Brompton Road? Is it possible, when you are no more an adventuress than people who read of the great green spaces and move between stucco and a desk?"

"Can I do no noble action, think no exalted thought,—and there was something else you said?"

"Away from the West with its parsons and smoke,
   Parsons and smoke, parsons and smoke,
   Where a man's not a man but a pig in a poke,
   A bird in a cage, or a pig in a poke."

"We have moods," said Mr. Balcony, "when the nobility of our thoughts moves us to tears, moods when we are convinced of the reality of goodness and long to increase the sum of it, as if it were a precious fluid swirling round the world, and bringing balm and peace to the tormented —something outside the mechanical scheme of things. And we aspire to sacrifice ourselves in some cause or other and be humbled, worshipping unknowns which are strong and beautiful, magnanimous, generous and kind. We melt with sympathy for all that we see and hear. Each little episode seems full of pathos and rich in meanings. We give thanks for the sunlight and the growth of grass, for clouds scudding past tall chimneys, for a bright curtain in a mean street and the voices of children. Our tears are fragrant as incense, and we cannot shed enough. Indeed, we enjoy ourselves and know it, and say with some boldness to the scientist, 'What are your laws of nature and survival-values to my beautiful thoughts?'"

"And what does he say?"

"He says, 'You are an elegant and useless breed, a by-product of creation, sterile as mules.'"

" And then ? "

" One day, we ask ourselves very secretly—perhaps when the fire has gone out, when the flags which we put up for the procession are taken down—very secretly we ask ourselves, like a lover at the first faint cooling of his love, whether our incommunicable certainties will see us to the end, whether the painfully won ecstasies of the devoted soul are anything more than a tickling of the skin or the feel of warmth on the spine, and whether of the mass of beauties which we have laboured so hard to experience, one particle will survive and bear fruit for us or others. And later, when we are moved by something, by music, a picture, a poem or the contemplation of a fine action, we ask ourselves the same question—and in the end we find we cannot rely on any of these narcotics."

" And what do we do then ? "

" We die with broken hearts—or we alter ourselves, put our trust in money and material possessions, or take to chess, acrostics and mathematics, or become still more changed and take a satanic pleasure in destroying our own natures, outraging ourselves so that others shall not outrage us."

" I should rather," said Gloria, " be a lady of fashion than a philosopher."

" So should we all."

" I mean, if we could think things are what we think them, it would be all right, wouldn't it ? "

" It would be, if we could control our thoughts. Suppose one finds fairly early that one's thoughts are unlikely to be gay ? "

" Then, one had better take to the sewing-machine.   But it can't be done all at once."

" Exactly.   The conversation of clever people is full of the unspoken.   Good night."

He went away, and Gloria, thinking of the view from her bedroom window in Lithe Street down which the taxis sped with lamps new-lit, gazed over the side of the boat at the dark waters.

> " Give me the East with its parrots and wines,
>   Parrots and wines, parrots and wines,
>   Give me the East with its concubines,
>   Its dancing-girls and concubines."

Lady Hoobrake, alone in the saloon, her hands resting without purpose on the yellow keys of the piano, leant back in her chair and listened with a happy smile.

(VIII)

Mr. Lloyd-Muce lay alone on the little bed in his cabin. Though he had waited for a long time, half-awake yet dreaming, for his wife to come in, on some errand which he could not now divine, he had ceased to expect her, and only wondered why the pain, which for some weeks had been the most faithful of his companions, had left him. Was it possible that he was going to get well? He went to sleep.

When he awoke he was in church, at a service whose origin (some rubric told him) had been the churching of women, though modern usage had altered its trend. The side-chapel, in which he was a prisoner, opened on to an array of candles and sanctuary lamps, while from a swinging censer just out of sight came the scent of warm wax, cedar-wood and cloves. Each time the censer swung to the left a voice said, "*Dominus vobiscum*," and when it swung to the right, another voice replied, "*Et cum spiritu tuo*." The constant repetition of these words was soothing and yet invigorating.

Meanwhile, the congregation, which had for many hours been assembling from all parts of the country, rose from its knees and cried out something with so loud a voice that the candle flames flickered upwards like serpents' tongues, tarnishing the gilt woodwork that formed the balustrade of the gallery. A bell tinkled and the curtain fell, but rose again to disclose taller candles, brighter lamps, and a vast safe with seven seals which the high-priest was about to break with a silver hammer. Now, in that safe were stored up the sins of the people.

While Mr. Lloyd-Muce was still on his knees, an olive-complexioned acolyte with an evil smile brought him a brown paper parcel. It contained, as he knew, his own sins. He could feel them through the paper, some round, some square and some triangular, and there was one very long and slender, with a sharp end, of which he was afraid. He opened the parcel and spread the sins out between his knees on the red hassock. Some were scarlet, some black and some green, and the sin with the sharp end alone was dull yellow. Neatly, as if arranging money or counters, he stacked the colours together, identifying each sin as he did so. But the sin with the sharp end he could not call to mind.

A bell rang, the candles burnt out and the curtain fell. Cups of coffee and biscuits were served on trays. The audience had come from afar and had brought neither wallets nor scrip. At a nod from the prompter, he walked, sins in hand, to the middle of the stage. When the curtain rose, he was wearing a black cassock. Then at a peal of angry bells the candles, high as palm-trees and waving in the wind, licked the roof with tall flames, and the high-priest, followed by an array of bishops, priests and deacons, came towards him.

"We will now," said the high-priest with a tailor's urbane smile, "try them on." And together they tried them on, each sin being applied like a poultice to that part of the penitent's body which had offended; and although some of

150

the applications were, in the presence of an audience, embarrassing, the procedure was simple and brief. As each sin touched the bare skin, it smarted, burnt a hole, and then melted, leaving no trace.

" It is because you have remembered them so carefully," said the high-priest, " that they fit so well."

Soon only the sin with the sharp point remained, but when the high-priest was about to press it into the flesh over the heart, Mr. Lloyd-Muce begged him to pause.

" I cannot call it to mind," he said. " Give me five minutes."

" Five minutes, and no more," said the high-priest, and pointed upwards to the roof which was ablaze.

Mr. Lloyd-Muce's mind became a blank. There was nothing in it, no memory, power of invention or thought. Drops of sweat trickled down his forehead.

The high-priest took the sin and pressed it into the flesh. Mr. Lloyd-Muce stiffened his muscles and gave a great cry; for the sin burnt like a strong acid and corroded the skin without melting as the others had done. The pain was unbearable. After an age the high-priest drew out the sin and waited ; but still no recollection came. Part of the burning roof fell with a crash into the font, killing a baby which was being baptized. The royal family left the building.

Once more the high-priest took up the sin and applied it. It burnt like a red-hot iron and made a wound stretching from the collar-bone to the groin. The victim, dripping with sweat and blood, fell on his face, and the high-priest paused in his work.

This happened seven times. The roof had now fallen in, and the black sky formed a background to innumerable whirling sparks which took the shapes of the faces and bodies of the damned who were in Hell, and fell on those of the congregation who still remained. And then the black sky itself opened and revealed the movement of phosphorescent cylinders and pistons and interlocking planes of light, while the roar of an immense machinery deafened the ears.

Then suddenly the high-priest, again drawing

out the sin, fell on his knees and gazed through the rent wall. The lights faded. The cylinders and pistons ceased to move. The sparks died and fell in a drizzling rain.

Over the damp grass, an angel was threading his way through the tombstones. The church-yard was quiet and beautiful, and suggested Christmas Eve in another century. The angel came up to Mr. Lloyd-Muce, and took him in his arms. There was something in the angel's hand that pricked slightly, like a needle or medical instrument.

" Why wait ? " asked the angel.

Mr. Lace, loitering, as was his wont, behind a ventilator, heard a low cry and a splash, and saw Mr. Balcony in white silk pyjamas walking away from the side of the deck.

(IX)

The approaching end of the long voyage some-what lessened the excitement which Mr. Lloyd-

Muce's death would otherwise have caused. The doctor testified that one of the drugs administered to his patient might have produced a sudden access of physical strength and mental derangement which would account for suicide. None of the sailors on duty had observed anything unusual during the night. Mr. Balcony did not press the inquiry. Mrs. Lloyd-Muce, beyond once referring to an unnatural sleepiness while she should have been on duty, said nothing. Mr. Lace, at this, proposed that the dregs of her coffee cup should be analysed, but the suggestion was ignored. The Major said, "Poor devil. Just as well." Mrs. O'Doyle had, after luncheon, a trance, during which many gratifying communications were made to her.

That afternoon, when the heat began to abate, Mr. Lace went to Gloria's cabin. She was sitting on her bed, and told him to come in.

For three minutes he looked at her in silence, the lines of his pale intellectual face full of a spiritual beauty.

"Gloria," he said, "we land to-morrow. Will you marry me?"

She smiled and shook her head. He noticed that she was again mending a white silk pyjama jacket, and his expression lost suddenly all charm.

"Those," he said, "are Mr. Balcony's pyjamas."

Again she shook her head.

"I tell you they are," he continued. "I've seen him in them."

"Really? When?"

"Last night, at two in the morning—after he pushed Mr. Lloyd-Muce overboard."

"Hilary, the heat has turned your head. If you say too much, the doctor will order you to be locked up."

He trembled.

"Ask Mrs. Lloyd-Muce why she fell asleep, then. She was doped."

"You talk like a penny-dreadful."

"She was drugged."

"Be very careful not to say these things in public. Make an effort to control yourself. Count six before you speak."

"These pyjamas——"

" They're mine, I tell you."

" Do you tear them every night ? "

" I tore them the night before you—visited me that time—and I tore them last night. The silk's worn out."

" The same pair——"

" No. Hilary, you are a maniac. Open that drawer. You will find four pairs of white silk pyjamas, all nearly worn out. I bought them all at the same time—wholesale and cheap. Go away and lie down."

He took a step forward.

" Gloria—do you love me ? "

" No. No. No."

" Then," he said, " I shall know what to do."

" That's more than I shall," she said, as he went out. And she burst into a dolorous snatch of song. One day more and the exotic trip would be half over. Was it possible to travel back by land ? She threw the pyjamas on to the floor, lay down and shut her eyes.

When she opened them, Mr. Balcony was sitting in her arm-chair.

" Mr. Balcony ? " she said tentatively.

" Let us ask each other a question," he said,
" and your turn first."

She looked at him with round eyes, and,
hardly knowing what she did, said suddenly :

" Did you murder Mr. Lloyd-Muce ? "

" Yes."

" Why ? "

" You have asked two questions where only
one is necessary."

For nearly five minutes she said nothing, and
looked at the ceiling. Then a flash of supreme
intelligence illuminated her.

" Because," she said, " his sufferings mean
nothing to you."

He smiled appreciatively.

" Eighth on the list, you remember ? ' Misfortunes of friends.' "

" Then why ? "

" Because," he said, his voice rising suddenly
to a high and mystical tone, " the day of my
perfection has not yet come. Do you not
understand that, if I were perfect, no one could
live with me ? Do you suppose that were I now
what I shall become, intercourse with me would

be possible ? The business of last night shows that I have gone a long way from what I was—I who would not step on black-beetles, I who was moved to tears by a withered flower, I who——"

He stopped suddenly, and continued in his normal bass :

" I am boasting—and despair of myself. There was a time, you must remember, when all I saw puzzled me, and when I had the sensation of living amongst people, not more intellectual, but shrewder than myself. Since then, I have enjoyed puzzling others. But it is a joy that I must leave behind. As for my question, it is this. Will you marry me ? "

" It is a question," he went on, as she said nothing, though he must have remarked a wave of delight that began to flow down her body and the involuntary preparation of an ecstatic smile, " which may seem more suited to a Surbiton drawing-room than to the edge of what Surbiton would call ' the dark continent.' But it is a last tribute that I wish to pay to the conventions, a last backsliding while it is still possible. You see, as the condemned ask for porridge and bacon and eggs, kidneys and mushrooms and lobster Newburg half an hour before execution, so I indulge an almost criminal fancy, and—but that is no matter. The Surbiton drawing-room insists that I should tell you my prospects, or rather yours. They are not bright, alas! I have spent all my money in hiring this boat. No, there is no trap; it will take you all back safe and sound and there will be nothing for you to pay. But my furniture in Lithe Street will have been sold to repay a loan from my bankers. Whatever surplus there is will be sent to you, but it will be almost nothing. For a few years I have been living—and living well—on my capital. So from me "— (his voice rose again to the mystic's sexless cry)—" expect no wealth, no material possessions and no fame."

" And when," she asked faintly, " should we be married ? "

" In a few days."

She held out her hand, which he kissed with much gallantry.

(x)

The same afternoon Major O'Hoone, who had long been eating and drinking excessively and taking no exercise, went to bed with all the symptoms of jaundice.

Mrs. O'Doyle, who had been warned in her trance that this mishap was the prelude to a greater joy, declared that, while the Major was abed, she would not disembark. Lady Hoobrake, appalled by the doctor's accounts of the noxious insects and tropical diseases against which in that part of Africa one had to guard, refused to go ashore, and her resolution was strengthened when she heard that Captain Buchanan intended to sleep on board so long as the ship was in port. She insisted too, that Aubrey should not endanger himself, and he promised to stay with her. Mr. Lace, on hearing of the Major's illness, complained of nausea and pains in the stomach, ate no dinner, and went to bed fearful of the gravest consequences. Later in the evening he felt better and asked the steward to beg Gloria to visit him. She came with pills, administered them, and told him of her intended marriage. Mr. Lace was then sick, and after ringing for the steward she went away ; nor, when he sent for her a second time did she go to see him.

Thus it was that shortly after breakfast on the following day, only four disembarked at the port of Gahta, Mrs. Lloyd-Muce, Aubrey (who came in secret), Gloria and Mr. Balcony. N'Gambi, the African servant, had gone ashore earlier in the morning.

The port was squalid and very much what an untravelled English woman would imagine a little port in Italy to be—and probably also very much what an untravelled Italian woman would imagine of a little port in Africa. It was flanked by dreary tumble-down buildings, scraggy trees the names of which Gloria did not know, and an expanse of sun-baked mud, in which grew a few parched clumps of weeds. In the distance were low houses of a dull red colour. As the travellers approached the quay in a little boat, they heard a shrill phrase of five notes which sounded as if blown on a reed-pipe.

"It is not to see the old churches or the scenery that I have come here," thought Gloria, as the boatman helped her up the gangway. But none the less, when her feet touched land once more, within herself she felt the opening of a door.

IV

THE MARRIAGE

THEY left Gahta the same morning by a little railway which was used for the transport of goods from G'Nuk. After going for some miles, the train stopped for half an hour in the shade of some enormous trees by the side of a stretch of green water, and N'Gambi served meat-cakes, nuts baked in syrup, fruits and a whitish wine. Mrs. Lloyd-Muce was as one who wished to see nothing. Aubrey talked to Mr. Balcony about roulette. The heat and the discomfort of the journey had taken the edge off such curiosity as Gloria might have had. Besides, she had a foreboding that she would soon learn more than she wished to know, and feared to prick the veil of the future by asking even so much as the name of a butterfly or a flower.

163

At sunset, the line which had been rising gradually, curved round a big valley, and on the far side of the valley, Gloria saw, bathed in flames of crimson, purple and gold, the city of G'Nuk, built on a precipice of rock, and resplendent, it seemed to her, with palaces and lofty towers of ivory and opal, crystal domes, bronze minarets and hanging gardens, from which flowed wreaths of tawny blossom, like the long hair of women bending downwards from a balcony. " It is," she thought, gazing over the dull expanse of stunted grass, stones, mud and sand, half-dried puddles and spiky evil-looking weeds, " like a city in an illustration to the Arabian Nights, a city built by a genie in a night, and containing all the treasures of the world. And it may be that I am to become the queen of it, mistress of a thousand slaves, fantastic jewels, spices and perfumes, rare essences distilled and purified for a hundred years in the burning sunlight, and that I shall be lapped in such bodily splendour, such refinements of comfort and physical sensation, that the activities of thought will appear a pale and savourless joy." And she compared herself to a flower plucked by the wayside, and placed in a costly vase full of a dubious elixir, becoming every day more indolent and more beautiful, and putting forth thick petals, and growing ranker and more poisonous within, till finally in the radiance of maturity the swollen bloom would dissolve in a welter of corruption and stain the air with a venomous fertility for miles around.

It may be that her thoughts took such a turn, because she did not wish to think of her marriage.

But meanwhile the train had moved on, and whether Gloria's vision of G'Nuk had been imagination or the result of the sunset, she now saw that the palaces and minarets were really squalid little houses or rocks jutting out of the precipice, and that the hanging gardens were built of smoke and dust.

When they arrived it was dark.

After a little delay, and a discussion between N'Gambi and some natives, they were conducted to a three-roomed bungalow on the outskirts of the town. In the middle room, which opened straight on to a stony track, they had supper by the light of two wretched lamps. Gloria wondered why Mr. Balcony had not made better provision for their comfort, but found only too many reasons why he should not have done so. After supper, while N'Gambi and another native went into the rooms on either side of the supper-room and took certain precautions against the dangers of the place, the four Europeans played bridge. Then they said good-night, the women going to the room on the left and the men to the room on the right. Their beds were uncomfortable rush mattresses. With hardly a word, Mrs. Lloyd-Muce went to sleep. Gloria's ears caught the sound of voices coming from the other bedroom, and, feeling jealous of a conversation in which she had no part, strove to gather what was being said. She heard, however, one sentence only. Mr. Balcony was speaking.

" I have never," he said, " made you any promise at all, and have too much on hand to bother with you. You may, as I told you, find gold or tin if you keep your wits about you, and if N'Gambi's brother takes a fancy to you, he may do something for you. He has no orders from me."

There were a few more murmurs and then all was silent in the bungalow. Outside there was from time to time a cry, whether of a man or an animal Gloria did not know. There was also a rustling against the woodwork which alarmed her, but it led to no unpleasant consequence. Then suddenly she heard the phrase of five notes which she had heard that morning at Gahta, blown on a reed-pipe. Time after time it was repeated, sometimes quickly, sometimes slowly and with a varying rhythm, though the notes and their sequence did not change. She wondered whether it was part of the normal colour of the place—like the taxis that rolled up Lithe Street on a summer night—or whether it had a more definite meaning for her which one day she would understand.

She awoke with a feeling of strain and fatigue, such as an Englishman might feel who had spent the day before with a French family who spoke only French, and realised that the ordeal of distorting his ideas to fit the feeble phrases at his command would soon begin again. She felt, absurd as it seemed, that it was her duty to become acquainted with the country which she was visiting, to master its fauna and flora, its geology, its economic situation, to pick up a few words of dialect. It was as if she had promised to deliver a course of lectures. Her two dominant impressions, heat and discomfort, seemed hardly adequate as memories. "No doubt," she thought, " I shall have willy-nilly more vivid memories than these, but they will not be suitable for the drawing-room." She kindled slightly at the thought, and banished it. " People won't want to know," she went on to herself, " how G'Nuk impressed me from the train, or what unpleasantly fascinating ideas I had yesterday afternoon. What they like is the American who can tell you more details about his home-town that I can about my wardrobe. But G'Nuk isn't my home-town." And at that point, she almost laughed to think what importance she was giving to the demands of the unknown questioners. It was the obligation of a nightmare, and she thought that she must have been dreaming to be so bothered. But she knew that the strain and fatigue which she still felt did not really proceed from this cause at all, and that her disappointments were harder to explain. The door which had seemed to open within her, when she set foot on African soil, was still but ajar.

N'Gambi came in, with no thought of the conventions, bringing two jugs of water, two cups of coffee and a few biscuits. Mrs. Lloyd-Muce awoke like a soldier under orders, ate, washed and dressed.

" You know," she said suddenly, " I go this evening."

" You go ? Where to ? "

" By train to Gahta, and the ship."

" Why ? "

" My duties will be over."

" What duties ? "

" As your chaperon of course."

Gloria laughed nervously and dropped the mug containing her tooth-water.

" Really ! I had never thought of that. But couldn't you stay all the same ? "

" My dear girl, this is hardly the place for politeness." And she rammed the Bellona hat on

her head like a panama. "A detestable woman,"
thought Gloria, and then remembered that it was
hardly the time for such thoughts. " Did he ask
you to come ? "

" Of course."

" And has he asked you to go ? "

" He told me to stay till to-day."

Was it possible, Gloria wondered darkly,
remembering Mrs. Lloyd-Muce's unnatural sleep
during the critical moment, and her acquiescence
in the "calamity," that they were in collusion ?
Had he mastered her—or paid her price ? After
this, one could hardly think of him as ineffectual.
But why a chaperon ? No doubt, it was a
caprice, a concession made by him to himself, a
husbanding of resources. Or a joke, a mystifica-
tion ? " It is hardly possible that he is consider-
ing me," she thought. " I have so often shown
myself prepared for—— And from him, one
cannot conceal one's wishes. Oh, if there is any
way in which I can be helped or strengthened,
may I find it soon ! " A pain shot through her
head and she was filled with terror for a
moment.

It occurred to her for the first time that Mr.
Balcony might be marrying her in order to do
himself a last piece of violence, to make himself
different from what nature had intended him to
be, a bachelor. The thought would have been
comic, had it not tallied so exactly with her
smattering of his philosophy.

Suppose Hilary was right, after all, and she
was dallying with a lunatic. It might be that she
was destined not to return, and that all the
talk of Lithe Street and the Knightsbridge Tube
the other evening was a piece of irony for an
imaginary audience. If one has romantic notions
it is a clear sign that one is unequal to their
fulfilment. People with interesting lives are all
callous and brazen-faced. They feel nothing.
Evidently her courage was only up to cinema
standard—a thriller in five acts, then a shrimp
tea with Tom and Florrie. But it was in vain
that Lady Jane Grey vaunted her slender neck.
The axe fell.

They breakfasted in the middle room. Mr.
Balcony was as urbane as a gentleman introducing

a party of ladies to the casino at Deauville. During the heat of the day, he said, Europeans ought to rest, but perhaps they would prefer to see the sights? Aubrey was pale and ill at ease. It was as if he too had bargained for something less.

They spent the morning trying to keep in the shade, visiting a few dilapidated shrines and the shops. Gloria bought some beads, sweetmeats and some little carved figures of improper designs. Aubrey bought two musical instruments. At noon, they visited the clergyman at the mission-hut; for although they were not in British territory a British mission had established itself. A young negress with flashing eyes said that the clergyman was out and would not be back for a few hours. They returned to the bungalow, had luncheon and rested. Gloria's apprehension grew, and she could not sleep. "If only," she thought, " it were like a cold plunge, and one could jump out or swim to shore, refreshed——" But it was not at all like that.

When the heat began to abate, they went to the mission-hut again. The clergyman was wearing a dirty suit of artificial silk. A marriage—

that day, he asked? It was impossible. There were formalities to comply with. An argument followed. "This lady (Mrs. Lloyd-Muce) must go back by the night train. There are no other women in our party." The clergyman was distressed. "Could they not all go back, and come again?" "No, they could not." "Had they no letters, no dispensation?" "None." "After all," said Mr. Balcony gently, "it is no great matter. We do not, I fear, attach as much importance to this service as you do." On hearing this the clergyman made a long protest, but in the end, when they were on the point of going, he gave way. "Let it never be said," he murmured, "that the strictness of our law has been a stumbling-block." And, lest the ardour of their passions should try them beyond their strength, he married Miss Swing and Mr. Balcony with great despatch. Then certain documents were signed by the spouses, witnessed by Aubrey and Mrs. Lloyd-Muce, and a scrubby clerk who represented the local Government, and given by Mr. Balcony to his wife, who put them in her hand-bag.

After this, they returned to the bungalow and drank a bottle of champagne, though nobody made any of the conventional speeches. Then they went to the station, where Mrs. Lloyd-Muce shook hands with them calmly, mounted the train, spread out a little mattress on the floor of a truck and lay down. A few minutes later the wretched little train moved away, and as it moved, Mrs. Balcony, less changed as yet than her new name might imply, waved her handkerchief with the despair of one who knows there can be no answer. Only Aubrey now was left to comfort her. On their way back to the bungalow she took his arm, but he disengaged it.

When they reached the bungalow, she said that she was tired, went to the women's room—now her room—and lay down. Mr. Balcony lay down in his room. Aubrey, whose tired eyes had begun to flicker with a deplorable curiosity, sat on the floor of the living-room and looked at a large map. A few minutes later, Gloria was startled by the entrance of N'Gambi. But he only came to keep an eye on those dangers which, though much hinted at, had so far not revealed

themselves.   He did, however, examine her feet.
She submitted without demur, and felt relieved at
having done so.   It did not occur to her to regard
him as a man.   When he had gone, she lay down
again, quivering with apprehension and incapable
of thought.

There was a knock on the door, which she
opened, to find that supper was ready.   They
ate and said little.

"And what," asked Aubrey suddenly, " shall
we do to-night ?   Three-handed bridge ? "

Hardly had he spoken, when he fell forward
on to the low table.   Gloria screamed.

" It's nothing," said Mr. Balcony, " just a
touch of the sun.   I'll see to him."

And he carried Aubrey into the next room,
and put him to bed.

" I can't eat," said Gloria to N'Gambi, and
signed to him to clear away.   He gave her a glass
containing a yellow liquid, and opened the door
of her room.   She went inside, put the glass by
the bed and lay down.   From time to time she
took a sip.

The effects of the drink were more than she could have hoped. Her panic gave way to an indifference which soon became actual serenity. She began to look upon herself as an experiment which one might watch through a key-hole or a chink in the curtains. She finished the draught and waited. She was still clear-headed, but in place of the apprehension which had tormented her, she had a self-assurance, a self-abandonment both novel and agreeable. And even when all that she had read or heard of marriage customs amongst savage races occurred to her, she felt no shrinking.

Some moments later—she had then no precise idea of time—the bedroom door opened quietly and three negresses came in. With gestures they invited her to strip. She did so, and after they had washed her with some slightly perfumed water, one of them emptied over her a little bottle of scent which reminded her of nothing so much as of white hyacinths. They then spread out a robe of many coloured veils—" the kind of dress," she thought, " that is donned only to be

176

doffed "—and wrapped it round her, arranging the draperies with subtle touches. Meanwhile one of them had covered the mattress with clean linen of surprising whiteness. For a moment she felt contemptuous of these trappings, which suggested too much the final scene in a charade on the word " harem." But to be a principal actor was something ; besides, the other principal was no doubt more contemptuous than she. What preparations, she wondered, was he making ?

And now, for the first time for many a day, now that the negresses had glided away and she was left attired in her strange raiment with a burning perfume-bowl in a corner of the dark room, she found herself thinking of intimate things which suffused her with a dreamy excitement, and a kind of bodily awe. Each moment as it passed seemed full of a grandeur that was almost tangible, a magnificence residing not so much in the mind as in the flesh. She would have liked to hear the jangling of bells, blowing of trumpets or beating of drums, to have had the night heralded by a tremendous fanfare, and celebrated by an immense procession. But even as the thought of a procession came to her, she remembered the procession seen from her balcony in Lithe Street and heard again, amid the cheering of the crowd at the very moment when the procession broke into the splendour of its fullest bloom, the words spoken by the man who had stood behind her—"It is life passing." And she began to fear that whether through caprice, indifference, or some more unfathomable reason, her husband would not after all come to her room. The triumph was over. She lay back on the white bed-covering and trembled.

Outside the reed-pipe played its phrase of five notes. From time to time something cried, whether man or animal she did not know. There was a rustling against the woodwork, and the shiver of a little breeze passed over the floor. She brushed the back of her hand against the veil which shrouded her wet eyes.

When she looked up, Mr. Balcony in his white silk pyjamas was standing in the doorway, holding a small lamp. He shut the door, set the lamp on the ground, straightened himself and smiled.

The following days were for Gloria less definite in their sequence. Till the day of her marriage, her life had seemed to flow onwards in accordance with the laws of time. There had indeed been here and there purple patches and pale patches, periods whose contours were now clear, now blurred. But there was about the whole a progress and a unity, a readiness to obey the divisions in a pocket-diary, that came to a sudden end. Events were now simultaneous instead of consecutive. Impressions lingered, vanished and returned with such complexity that present, past and future became indistinguishable. And in this labyrinth—a labyrinth of sun and shadow, plains and hills, broad waters and enormous trees—she had to guide her only the slenderest of threads.

They set out, next day, upon a journey with a retinue of natives. Gloria asked her husband where they were going, and why, and when they would return, but he gave her no clear answers. In the middle of the day the heat overcame her and she fainted. When she revived, N'Gambi gave her a drink which made her sleep till night-fall. Two natives carried her in a closed litter. That night they camped at the edge of a forest. She and her husband shared a small tent.

In the morning N'Gambi gave her the drink again, and again she fell asleep, to awaken in the tent which was on a hillock beside a broad stretch of water. The same happened each day, and of the journey she had no memories beyond the glimpses which she caught of the country where they rested. Meanwhile, of her husband she had nothing to complain, save that at certain moments he would seem to be unaware of her presence and would look abstractedly at nothing, as if his thoughts were deep and incommunicable. And in this mood, if he spoke, it was to himself rather than to her, and in a high-pitched voice which, the more she heard it, filled her with an obscure fear. But each time, the trance, or whatever it was that possessed him, soon passed, and the warmth of his normal bass would reassure her.

One night, after she had slept for two hours,

she awoke with her brain full of an unusual alertness and the feeling of apprehension. She opened her eyes, and in the moonlight which was diffused inside the tent, she saw her husband sitting on the ground, his shoulders leaning against the slanting canvas and his head bent forward. His eyes were shut but his lips moved as if he were telling imaginary beads. His pyjama jacket was unbuttoned and had fallen about his waist. For a few minutes she watched him, and then stretched out her arm, stroked the side of his hair, his ear and neck, and let her hand rest on his left shoulder. He opened his eyes and looked at her without seeming to know who she was.

" To-morrow," he said suddenly in shrill tones, like an aged prophetess delivering oracles from the recesses of a vast cave, " your journey is over, and mine begins. Your journey is over, and mine begins."

He repeated the words, at intervals, three or four times.

" Are we," she asked, " going back to the ship to-morrow ? "

"I," he answered slowly, "am not going back. You will go back without me, and try as you will, you will never find me again, never see me again, or hear from me again."

She withdrew her arm and lay watching him in silence. Two tears trickled down his cheeks, and he rubbed them away slowly with his fingers.

"These," he said, "are the last tears I shall shed."

At this she began to weep herself, and turned her face downwards on to the cushion which served as pillow, so that he should not see her. When she looked up again she saw him, half-naked as he was, creeping out through the opening of the tent.

For a few seconds she lay too bewildered and miserable to move, and then with desperate courage got up, put on a pair of light slippers and a thin wrap, and hurried after him. The tent was in a corner of a level piece of land surrounded on all sides by big trees whose thick leaves hung like metal discs in the motionless air. Following his white figure, she crossed the clearing and forced her way into the forest. Like an agile old woman he darted round the tree-trunks and scrambled through the net-work of tendrils that formed the undergrowth. Still she pursued him, her body scratched and bleeding and her eyes straining for the flicker of light which told her where he was. But the flicker grew fainter and died away. For a while she continued in what she surmised was the same direction, but her steps became slower and her arms could hardly force herself a passage, and at last she stopped by the side of a small clear pool. Beyond the pool a huge tree, struck by lightning, lay horizontally, and through the gap which it should have occupied the moonlight struck the water.

Exhausted, she sank on the wet ground, her face bending over the water's edge. Deep down, a pale ghost of herself looked up at her with staring eyes. She knew that she was lost, but as yet felt no fear. She knew, however, that the fear was not far off and dreaded it, as one dreads an approaching ordeal. The water was smooth and silvery, though a gentle rippling of the surface showed that there was a spring. She stretched out a bare arm and lowered it gradually into the cool depths, as if it were the root of a plant coiling down through the earth. Then she stretched out her other arm, and let it fall with its own weight, while her head bent forwards till she felt the lapping of the water on her forehead.

"You will meet your love at a place with trees round it."

The words were Mrs. O'Doyle's and spoken ten thousand miles away. " The drowning," she thought, "are supposed to live their whole lives again in the last few seconds. If they are rescued soon enough, they can be revived. It is the dead coming to life again ; for by the time one is unconscious the struggle is over, and one might as well have died." She shut her eyes.

When she opened them, she was in her husband's arms, the white canvas of the tent rising round her.

"Where," she said, after some minutes, " have you been ? How did you——? "

" I have been nowhere," he answered in his bass voice.

Dreamily she felt for her wet clothes, but he had taken them off. Then she looked at her hands and wrists. They were scarred but not bleeding.

" Then how did I——" she began, but he closed her mouth gently with his right hand, and with the other stroked her neck and hair.

The next day they set out as usual, but when N'Gambi offered her the wonted draught as she composed herself on the litter, she drank only half of it, and poured away the remainder while he was not watching. Thus it was that she awoke to find that though the litter was resting on the ground, the sun was still high in the sky, and there was no sign of the tent's having been pitched for the night. The ground was marshy, and tall reeds, many of which bore a pale bluish flower, surrounded the litter. In the distance there was a vast sheet of water whose waves splashed against a muddy bank. For a few moments Gloria thought that they had reached the sea, and looked for the ship on which she supposed they were to embark.

Instead of the ship, however, she saw four or five small boats drawn out of the water on to the mud, and a great concourse of natives whirling this way and that, with raised knives that glittered in the air. Some of them beat drums, while others played on pipes and stringed instruments, shouted and jangled together metal chains.

Like a sleep-walker, Gloria rose from the litter, the fierce sunlight beating down upon her head, and stood on a little tufted patch of rising ground, covered with reeds and their blue flowers. Neither her husband nor N'Gambi were at hand, nor could she see the bearers of her litter. For a few moments a white cloud of smoke or steam hid the throng by the water's edge.

Then the cloud thinned, and she could see in the middle of the errant throng a group of natives whose dress and bearing somehow distinguished them from all the others. From their movements and gestures she first judged them to be women, but afterwards felt less assured of this. They seemed to be engaged upon some earnest con-

versation amongst themselves and paid no heed
to the others. Then the members of the group
shifted their positions and revealed her husband
standing in the centre. He was wearing a loose
white robe which was strange to her. For some
minutes, during which her sight grew more confused, he seemed to be conversing with them.
Then suddenly he fell on to his knees, and one of
the group came up to him and began to shave his
head and upper lip.

These facts she noticed in the dispassionate
and mechanical way in which a gambler might
notice the fall of the cards which brought him to
final ruin, or a man, whose life depended on a
rope, might watch the strands breaking one by
one.

Then the group closed in, and she could see
her husband no more. The music ceased and the
dancers became motionless, and held themselves
rigidly as if turned to stone. The reeds and
grasses stood bristling and erect. The waters
seemed to have receded from the shore, baring
a long stretch of steaming mud, while flames of
brass, flung outwards from the sun, swept down

upon the desolate country and scorched it to black dust.

And the earth itself rose up from under her feet and struck her between the eyes, and as she fell head foremost into the void, she saw far off the flashing of a curved knife in the air and heard a cry like the death-cry of a bull.

V

RECOIL

THE whistle blew three times, and the *Percy* steamed slowly through the narrow entrance of the harbour into the ocean, carrying back to England only five of the nine unsalaried passengers who had made the outward voyage. Of these five, two were on deck watching the disappearance of the port, whose familiarity fatigued them.

"At last," said Lady Hoobrake, leaning back in her deck-chair and sighing.

"It's demoralised us all," said Mr. Lace, fearing that his voice was like a clergyman's. "It's detached us from the main stream of life. In these days—it's retrograde. We've been building up little stories for ourselves, and pandering to unwholesome personal emotions. We've

189

lost—or some of us have—all sense of duties and real values."

"Ah," said Lady Hoobrake, who was only half-listening, "but when you got over your bilious attack, you had your little trips on shore, hadn't you? Captain Buchanan saw you with a fluffy little black——"

"Of course I've been on shore," he interrupted rudely. "What else could I do? I'd read all my own books and written till I couldn't hold the pen. Nothing to read in the ship's library except detective stories and other trash. The only way to keep sane was to go on shore. Thank God, I haven't lost my head—like some of us. Buchanan's tattle means nothing to me."

How brusque he was, she thought, how old-mannish, how changed, all of a sudden—"puritan *faute de mieux*," as Aubrey had described someone.

"La, sir," she said aloud, by way of contrast apeing a character in an eighteenth-century biography which she had once skimmed through, "I don't press you. Each man's business is his own. I'm not strait-laced."

He found it impossible not to continue his lecture.

"When we get back," he went on, "we shall find that things haven't been standing still. Society's about to take a big leap forward. With economic conditions such as they are, we cannot hope for stability. Indeed, we do well not to hope for it. Nothing is more destructive to an organism than too much repose. I see big things ahead."

"Come, come, Mr. Lace. I hardly see you as a leader of the *canaille*. You'll do better to keep to your articles on the spoiling of the countryside."

She yawned a farewell to the promontory which had been too long the limit of the world, and turned her eyes to her book. Mr. Lace, who had only spoken to her because he was tired of not speaking to her, strolled round the deck twice and went to his cabin, where he intended to write. The return voyage would be less odious than the voyage out, he reflected. No Balcony, no Mrs. O'Doyle, no Major. They would be a quiet, if dull, little party. And that wretched girl wouldn't trouble him. She had behaved as badly as she could, but it had been very foolish to imagine that anyone so scatter-brained, so lacking in ideals and, indeed, all qualities except those which drove her to snatch at capricious pleasures, could ever have been suitable for him. She had shown herself as great a lunatic as the lunatic she'd eloped with. She had had her deserts, and there should be no " I told you so." But unless she pulled herself together, there wouldn't be much room for her in the new Europe. It might even be for the best, he thought bitterly, if she didn't live to reach England again. She was in a pretty bad way, the doctor said. Presumably the doctor was a fully qualified man. But was it quite safe to trust him when he said that Mr. Lloyd-Muce's trouble couldn't possibly have been communicated to his wife ?

And for nearly an hour Mr. Lace occupied his mind with that unpleasant but important problem.

Aubrey, brushed and scented, spick and span

in white samite, carried some maps to his mother's feet.

" I have," he said, " made good. And now that I have, I'm confident that when we reach England I shall find myself Uncle ffawkes's heir."

" O God," said Lady Hoobrake, " if it were true ! But I still think you ought to do something about your Spanish."

" I deserve," he went on, " everything I get. I can't describe the miseries I endured—bad food, bad smells, bad beds, stings, bites, blisters."

" I'm a little frightened of that Major."

" How ? "

" Suppose he finds your concessions ? "

" He won't. Besides, A'Kimbo will see to him."

" Who is that ? "

" I told you. N'Gambi's brother, but by another father—the one I found myself with when the other birds had flown. A'Kimbo is devoted to me. He called me ' Great White Chief.' "

" I can hardly believe that."

" He did, and many other names too."

" But all you've got is a box of samples and a few papers."

" No one ever has any more than that. The mine shall be known as Aubrey Kimbo Tin, Limited."

" Tell me, Aubrey, did Miss Swing really marry Mr. Balcony ? "

" Yes. I was a witness."

" So we shall have to call her Mrs. Balcony ? "

They were very quick, she thought, as Aubrey walked away, and speculating as to the conduct of her own romance, she took a long draught from the glass beside her chair.

Mrs. Lloyd-Muce sat outside the door of the cabin which had been her husband's. The sunlight glancing off the brim of her Bellona hat struck the tip of her nose and chin. Such of her face as was in shadow, had a look of indomitable calm. She had with her a volume of Johnson's *Lives of the Poets*, a loan from Mr. Lace. But she held the book upside down.

After the unnatural lucidity of many a fevered

trance, shadow-chases over gigantic obstacles, timid triumphs and bravely borne dismays, Gloria's waking self, like a night-light new lit in the middle of a dark corridor, trembled into flame, waxed and waned and steadied its feeble ray.

She was attended by the doctor and a gaunt stewardess. Her first questions they parried or left unanswered. But when they might have told her some of the truth, she was too wise to ask anything of them ; for she knew that she had more secrets than they.

A letter from Mrs. O'Doyle lay by her pillow. She opened it, when she had watched it, as if it were a live animal, for two days.

" Gloria, darling, it had to be, and we're deserting you. If it weren't that I know you'll come back safe and sound, I wouldn't have done it. Maybe it'll not come as a surprise to you to know that my varied (and always romantic) career has taken yet another turn. This time it's the hotel business. The Major (who's now feeling fitter than he ever did in his life) and I are now proprietors of the Excelsior Hotel of Gahta and the Universe. The port, you know, is in a fair way of development, and when they open the new road, we shall have no end of a slap-up. (The engineers' drinks alone should bring in a small fortune.) To be sure, it isn't a very splendiferous affair as yet. But the hotel's only a beginning. We've hands for everything we can lay them on. There's money in it, love, and we'll come back as Nabobs. If you'd like to put a hundred or two into the concern, you're quite welcome. In fact, capital's a bit short.

"But now, my love, I won't bother you any more with your humble servants. What of yourself? Fine times you've had in the jungle, I'll be bound, and you've come back with bags full of rubies and emeralds and a rope of pearls that would girdle the belly of an elephant. You won't forget me when you get back home?

"And if, by the by, you're not too busy fitting yourself up in Carlton House Terrace, you might send your third secretary—and you'll have a pretty taste in secretaries, my dear—round to Rosabel and tell her to send out my black trunk.

She can sell the old candlesticks and the mirror —or perhaps you'd like them? They're genuine antiques, and we've had them in the family since the fifteenth century. Alec Raven always said they'd be cheap at two hundred, but you can have them for seventy. And, then, if it isn't bothering you, there's Adele, who's got my jade earrings and a pawn-ticket for my turquoise pendant. If you could see her and tell her to——"

At this point Gloria laid aside the letter, just as she would during those days lay aside her thoughts as she began to think them, her projects as she began to form them.

She remained in her cabin two days longer than her health required. When she met her companions, she was slow to recognise them, and smiled guiltily, as one does when asked about the dangerous illness of a friend.

The doctor, turned soul-healer, warned her of what was to come.

" Your loneliness," he said, " which is now only a gnawing pain, will in a few days become almost unbearable. Each day you will be amazed that you can suffer more than you did the day before. Then slowly it will die down, and leave behind nothing but a narrow scar."

"If ever," she vowed, when she was alone, "I cease to remember him, or suffer because I haven't him any longer, may the marrow melt in my bones, my tongue rot in my mouth and my eyeballs burst from their sockets." She had read something like it, but was by no means insincere.

All the familiar sights of the ship, places where they had sat, strolled or talked together, spared her nothing. And in her cabin there was the window through which he had looked dispassionately during Mr. Lace's outburst of violence. To hide it, and to prevent other faces from peering in, she kept the curtains drawn.

For hours each day, when sitting on deck, eating, answering her fellow-travellers, waiting to go to sleep, she went over in her mind all that had happened to her between her arrival at Gahta and the moment of what was called her sunstroke. The blurring of a scene or the misplacing of a detail filled her with frenzy, as if she were an old acrobat who makes a slip while practising an exercise that once came easily to him. Yet, each time she reconstructed these events, although her idea of their sequence and importance became increasingly clear, the visual image became less and less distinct. In the end, she could no longer see even the faces and gestures of those who had most constantly been with her, but had to evolve the picture laboriously from memories, as it were, already memorised. And these shed no sudden light upon the brain, but gave a grudging information, like a big dictionary through which one searches for a half-forgotten word.

Meanwhile, the great moments, the big pictures, were overlaid with spurious and fantastic details. Thus it was that, when her thoughts turned to the few minutes which preceded the end of her adventure, she saw no lake or inland sea, no wilderness of reeds and bluish flowers, no figures dancing on the muddy shore, but Aubrey waving to her from the top of a tall tree, herself pulling on a pair of gloves, and her father in his top-hat waiting impatiently for her to get into the carriage which was to drive them to

Hurlingham. And she had to remind herself deliberately that not one of these incidents was true.

"You can," said the doctor, "always write your memoirs." He had met her coming out of Mr. Balcony's cabin where she had found nothing but clothes—no letters, no personal papers, no photograph.

The next day she constructed a tedious but elementary cipher, and began to write. At first she made mistakes, could not read what she had written, and almost tore up the pages. Then she grew more skilful, aroused her memories to white heat and filled the gaps in them with imaginative deductions. It was a record without reticences or euphemisms. When she re-read it, she felt that she was reading about someone else. Then she learnt to visualise what she had written, bound it up with her past, and suffered because it could never be again.

Lady Hoobrake gave Gloria a lazy sympathy. Her questions, put as soon as it was decent to put questions, were answered so incoherently, that she assumed that Mr. Balcony, engaged upon a dubious financial project, had quickly tired of his wife, sent her back to the boat when she became ill, and taken to negresses. Mr. Lace was often minded to offer consolation and advice, but decided that the very personal nature of Gloria's trouble did not merit much consideration from those who thought not individually but collectively. Besides, he argued, taking no little pleasure in the vast broad-mindedness of this thought, to the retrograde temperament the fundamentals of progress give cold comfort. And he lamented that Gloria was never to have the full vision which came to Christina Alberta at the four hundredth page.

Aubrey's curiosity could not be satisfied. He questioned all who could answer him, except Gloria, and learnt nothing. He spied upon her continually, and, when he found that she was writing, crept into her cabin and searched for the manuscript. Had he found it, he would have soon been able to transcribe it. His own story he told repeatedly. His hearers agreed that it was uncommonly romantic and showed no little personal address.

Mrs. Lloyd-Muce's story, on the other hand, was unadorned. " They saw me off," she would say as if uttering a reprimand, " after the wedding. We were staying in cheap lodgings. Whether they moved to better quarters later, I don't know." Mr. Lace talked to her frequently. She seldom answered him. But when his ear ached, she prepared the poultice.

Meanwhile it became evident to the travellers that the ship must have loitered unnecessarily on the outward voyage ; for already, though it was still hot, there was an invigorating quality in the air, and the days, paradoxical as it seemed to Lady Hoobrake, grew rapidly longer. It was time to look ahead.

It was a calm evening, and the *Percy* was passing the coast of Portugal.

" When I get back," said Aubrey, " I shall go straight to the city and float my concession."

He had stooped to playing deck quoits with Mr. Lace, a game at which neither excelled.

"When we get back," said Mr. Lace, "there will probably be no city. When you reach port, you'll be given a suit of Government clothes and ordered to learn a trade at a Government school. The red flag will fly over Buckingham Palace, and we shall have a national opera."

And each, as in his turn he missed the mark, made the argument more bitter.

Gloria, sitting at a distance behind them, could hear not only their voices, but also Lady Hoobrake accompanying Captain Buchanan at the piano in the saloon, and a faint music that drifted up from the crew's quarters, a wayward serenade of concertinas and plucked instruments.

"When we get back," she thought, "the lilacs and laburnums will no longer be in bloom. We shall have autumn flowers, asters and chrysanthemums and holly-hocks and rotting stalks in the herbaceous borders. The paths will be littered with brown leaves. It will be a time of sparkling grass, big moons and mists, the beautiful ne'er-do-well season when life runs to seed and squanders itself in perverse unfruitful charms."

Then her thoughts turned to Lithe Street, the

early drawing of the curtains, the arc-lamp gleaming through the chinks between, the passing taxis with their shut windows. Seeing herself once more in the shop at the corner, she looked in imagination out into the street. Her husband was walking slowly from No. 38 towards Brompton Road. When he saw her through the plate-glass, he smiled. He was as she first knew him—as others would still remember him—the gentle military figure, who, they surmised, had " had a disappointment," one who could grasp an idea more readily than a fact, and therefore puzzled fools, one who looked on and smiled when he should have acted—but was always very kind. . . .

For this she had once taken him. She had smiled with a happy indulgence at his mystery, had flattered herself that she saw through his reticence, fathomed his need for sympathy. She had planned a whole idyll on these lines. Almost she had seen herself running about the house and singing snatches of light song, while he sat in his chair—these preliminary fancies of hers had made him very old—and watched her proudly and said something very clever which she tried to understand. It would be, she had thought, a comfort to have him there, noticing philosophically all their little follies, the incarnation of the larger view, no match for the world but yet above it, irresolute but serene. It was as if his presence would have given a purpose to their activities, a mellowness to their crudeness, to their shrill airs a solemn harmony.

This was long ago, when she had thought of herself in the plural, as being with others, part of a life outside, not isolated, not detached. For even then, he was not what he seemed. He had torn to pieces the pattern of that ineffectual old age, foreseeing it in all its wretchedness. He had dismissed the tender virtues, scorned the full and brimming heart, senile romance with its brave smiles and tears. This was no martyr, no theoretic angel come at the cost of torment to hand on the humanitarian torch. An ogre, rather, with his own notions of nirvana.

Indeed, it was not to become the trilling child-wife of a benign old man that she had followed his destiny. She had seen him in a few weeks shed half his years, grow daily in virility and strength; she had marked all the outward and visible signs of his progress. Had he not, without effort, gathered the party together, divined the future of each of its members, dominated them all, subdued Aubrey, terrified Hilary, quelled the Major's rowdiness, reduced the swaggering Buchanan to the level of a servant? Had not all their actions magnified him, tended together towards the accomplishment of his purpose? And yet, when he had succeeded, and become all that she could conceive his wishing to become, he had moved still farther from the mould of common clay, and taken, with her as witness, a step into the darkness, which now veiled him.

At that moment she knew that she was thankful for the past as it had been, and wished for nothing changed.

She paused in her reasoning, and thought idly of her companions on the boat, all of them with little stories of their own—the pale intellectual who had thought himself her lover till he found

a soul - mate with a Bellona hat—the elderly
couple united in the bureau of a tropical hotel—
the old lady with " county " connexions drawn
over the bottle to a swash-buckling impostor—
the young wastrel who " made good in the dark
continent," and would thenceforth be able to
have a bathroom built of purple marble and a
valet in pale green livery. They had had, on
board, disease, hysteria, murder, attempted rape
—" events of a life-time " in plenty—stories fit
for the cinema. She had, even, her own, and
when at home they asked her, she would tell
them how in Africa she saw this and that, made
an instructive expedition to the ruined temple,
shot her lion or tiger, observed the wonderful
progress of our missionaries. "A great change
from London. Have you come back the same ?
Will you, do you think, settle down again
quickly ? " But the real story was not of facts
but of an idea.

Stories fit for the cinema. The cinema was
over and they were going back to a shrimp
tea with Tom and Florrie. Their laughter
would echo through the basement, call a peep

from the policeman through the iron railings, a grin, a wagging finger. " Girls will be girls."

She was reminded suddenly of a night soon after the new year, when she had been walking joylessly near Portman Square. As she approached one of the large houses, the front door opened and a young man in evening dress, wearing a false nose, let out a young woman in an orange opera-cloak. She had heard the girl saying, " It's been a simply ripping party. I don't think I've ever laughed so much before. I *have* enjoyed myself." The girl repeated the sentence twice, and at some remark from her friend broke into peals of laughter so violent that she had to go indoors again—either to recover herself or to continue.

And it had seemed to Gloria that all the people she knew were then convulsed with laughter, and that she would be lost unless she could laugh too, not at wit or humour, but at nothing, and acquire suddenly a new sense of the silliness of things. It had seemed that salvation lay in mocking wisdom, duty and beauty, not by any intellectual feat of parody, but by a brutish impulse to pure laughter, which alone could convert all creeds and codes, assertions and denials into folly. Then indeed there would be no problems. "I don't think I've ever laughed so much before. I *have* enjoyed myself." Pure laughter—not the brave jest of the soldier in the trenches, of the widow when the cruse runs dry, not the literary facetiousness of the high-brow or healthy Elizabethan fun. Pure laughter—at mere shapes and sounds—at nothing—a negation of all faculties save one. Yet, as she had walked home that night she had wondered, "What of pain? It is hard to see silliness in the pain of one's own body."

She looked round the deck. Mr. Lace and Aubrey had finished or abandoned their game and gone inside. The music still floated through the clear air, the different sounds now rising and now falling like liquids of different colours poured into the same bowl, but not yet entirely mingled. There was Captain Buchanan by the piano in the saloon, the guitar, the dulcimer and the concertina in the crew's quarters, and the sailor with the beautiful voice, who sang to many tunes one line only :

"Ah, bear in mind, this garden was enchanted!"

Once more, she began to think, this time may be with a deliberate wistfulness, of how when they got back to England, the lilacs and laburnums would no longer be in bloom, how the first fog would soon envelop Lithe Street, and she would sit by the window, looking out at noon on to a cold darkness.

And yet the procession, which she had watched and seemed to be watching still, had passed that window. They had sat there together in the sunlight, while banners waved, the crowd cheered and pressed forward, and the whole procession blossomed, like a flower opening suddenly, into a vision of colours and sounds, strength and speed, each moment a braver array. And as it passed with swifter rhythm, louder fanfares, a voice had said in the distance, "It is life passing," and immediately one realised that the street was a severed artery and the procession life-blood spurting from the body, pent up no longer in frail and narrow veins, but squandering itself in a supreme jet that stabbed the bright air and fell. But the noise of the cheering grew fainter, and the watchers turned away their pale faces. Nor was anyone left to see the tall surgeons in their long white robes, coming at dusk to the prone body and binding up its wounds, or how when they found their skill of no avail, they washed their hands of the blood, smiled at one another as they prepared the body for burial, and carried it between them to a wild and stony place in a distant country, where, having dug a deep pit between two boulders, they covered it with rubble and sand and sharp flints . . . . clamoured in high piping voices for the sun that was to be their lover. And presently when they had waited for hours in the darkness, a faint light broke over the mountains and very slowly a bright disc rose above the topmost crag and sailed into the middle of the sky. Then the pale virgins felt once more the blood trickling through their veins. Their voices grew richer and more passionate, their gestures warmer and more

amorous, till at the moment when each expected
for herself the fulfilment of a beatific mystery,
a whisper passed among them and they under-
stood that it was no sun whose rays illumined
them, but the moon, the chaste and cruel moon,
their elder sister. . . .

She was awakened by the gaunt stewardess
tapping her on the shoulder and telling her that
it was late and very cold. Without speaking, or
feeling the cold, or the stiffness of her limbs,
Gloria went to her cabin and began to undress
slowly. But when she judged that there was no
more danger of meeting the stewardess, she took
her manuscript out of its hiding-place, crumpled
it up, and ran out on to the deck, intending to
throw it overboard; for there was a space of
deck between her cabin-window and the side of
the boat that might have falsified her aim. When
she saw the sea, however, and something white
floating on it, which might have been an old
newspaper thrown out at that moment by one of
the crew, she paused, went back to her cabin,
took up a green bottle a quarter full of liquid

soap for the hair, emptied it, and rammed the manuscript sheet by sheet down the neck. Then she put the cork in firmly, sealed it on with all the sealing-wax she had, and hurried furtively on to the deck again. When she reached the side of the boat she hesitated, passing the bottle from hand to hand, till suddenly a voice close to her ear whispered, "Why wait?" She looked round quickly, but saw nothing but the door and window of the cabin, which on the outward voyage had belonged to Mr. Lloyd-Muce. It had since been offered to Mr. Lace, but he had refused it. Both the door and window were shut, and no light was burning within. Besides, the voice had been close to Gloria, by the balustrade. "It must have been here," she thought, "that he threw him overboard," and she turned again towards the sea, took the bottle in both hands, and threw it with all her strength downwards into the water. In her fancy she could see it bobbing up and down a few yards from the ship.

Half an hour later when she was in bed, she still felt that her story was following faithfully behind, keeping pace with the rhythm of the engines and the rhythm of her thoughts—"a story not of facts but of an idea." But whether she had learnt anything from it, or read its lesson aright, she could not determine, before she fell asleep.

The next day there was at dawn a cold breeze, which by noon had become a rainy wind. Rolling waves broke against the side of the boat, and the passages and cabins were filled with a chilly freshness. Windows and portholes were shut one by one. Those who paced the deck wore raincoats or mackintoshes, and longed suddenly for tea by the fire, drawn curtains, hot pipes, and the glow of electric light through silk shades.

They reached England, and said good-bye to the doctor and Captain Buchanan, who were remaining on board. Lady Hoobrake's farewell, which Aubrey watched narrowly, contained no warmth, and when, in reply to a muttered hope of reunion, the doctor looked from her to the captain and shook his head, she made no protest, but went in search of a suit-case; for she was sick with hope deferred, and northern winds had brought a prudent resignation.

The five visitors disembarked, and after they had waited on wet quays and a wet platform for an hour and a half, the London train arrived. They could not avoid getting into the same compartment.

Mr. Lace distributed newspapers. There was nothing in them to show that General Harrier had died or that a revolution had broken out, and the first piece of news to be proclaimed publicly was that the name " Leatherhead " used to be spelt and pronounced " Leret." The announcement was made by Lady Hoobrake after a silence of ten minutes. Before she had time to read further, Mr. Lace gave them an account of the publishers' advertisements—a new Wells, a new George Moore, *Priapus, or the Future of Love*, and a work full of promise by a young woman who lived in Bloomsbury. Aubrey, intent on the financial page, said that the price of tin was rising.

Gloria, who did not read where the hips that autumn would be worn, though the page was open in front of her, shut her eyes and rested her head in the corner of the carriage. Her imagination sped through the floor, into the revolving wheels, from the wheels into the lines and along them backwards to the wind-swept buffers by the sea. And, as if she had left the draughty station and gone into the port, she saw the waves breaking spitefully upon the noisy shore, and beyond them a heaving greyness that stretched till it met a gloomy sky. Nor was it long before she saw, first as a faint speck on the horizon and then more clearly, a green bottle bobbing up and down with red sealing wax plastered over the neck. As she looked, it spun backwards, and leapt, like a fish jumping a waterfall, over the horizon's edge. But her thoughts could still follow it, and she knew how it would be carried along the *Percy's* outward course to the coast of Africa, and thence even farther, south and north and east and west, from China to Peru, not once nor twice, but many times completing the circle of the earth.

Yet, some day—and it would be a day while she was still living—a visitor on the beach at

Brighton or Bexhill, Margate, Scarborough, or chilly John o' Groats, would find it high and dry among the pebbles, pick it up carelessly and make as if to throw it at a prancing dog and notice that it was sealed. And inevitably the unhappy contents, pulled out and smoothed, thumbed at the pub, shown to the parson, sent to a museum or professor or cipher-expert at the Foreign Office, would be made known. Day by day conjectures and deductions—" the writing is not more than two years old," " the events depicted cannot have occurred before 1921," " the style indicates an imaginative but illiterate woman of the middle classes "—would narrow down the trail, and in the end, after a thousand ill-informed letters had been written to the papers, and a thousand false clues had been investigated, the truth would be revealed. Reporters and photographers would come to Lithe Street, a crowd, like the crowd that had watched the procession, would gather in Brompton Road, a detachment of police would be sent to keep order.

Early that morning, warned before daybreak

by a premonition of disaster, she would have gone downstairs and seen that the shutters of the little shop were tightly closed, that the shop-door was bolted with its two bolts, chained and locked, that the catches on all the windows were fastened. From that time onwards, too terrified to eat or sleep or read, she would be sitting in the back room. But even there, there was no safety. At first a confused murmur, then louder and more articulate, the voices of the mob, the voices of humanity, would echo through the house and clamour for her. " We know," they would say, " we know, we know." And they would cry out a travesty of her husband's secret, mock her by mocking him. " The man who was afraid of his own nature . . . the man who tried to make himself different from what he was . . . different from others . . . different from us . . . the man who thought he was above nature. . . . Unnatural! Unnatural! Unnatural! Have him out ! . . . Have her out ! . . ." Some of them, too, would know by heart sentences from the diary and would distort them and shout them aloud. " How long now is it since you . . . ?

Don't you wish now you could still . . . ?
So you did . . . this and this and this . . . ? "

Through the brick wall came the voices, a
babel of obscene words, jeers, threats, and howls
as of wild beasts, and finally a great cry in unison,
" Shame ! Shame ! Have her out ! Strip her,
whip her, stone her, burn her, burn her, burn
her . . . ! " and the foundations of the house
shook and the walls came tumbling down.

The dripping window had slipped, and Mr.
Lace, trying clumsily to fasten it, trod on her toe.
He apologised and said, " I think I've caught
cold."

As he sat down, Mrs. Lloyd-Muce took a
thick coat from the rack and spread it over his
shoulders.

Gloria, noticing her feet as a result of Mr.
Lace's apology, found that she was pressing them
against the floor with all her strength, as if the
whole world were a slimy worm that she was
squashing flat.

She did not speak till the train reached the
London station, and then, when it had almost

stopped, she said quickly to her four companions, "I've decided to call myself Miss Swing still. If you don't mind, I'd rather you didn't use my other name or mention it to anyone." Before any collective reply could be made, she was on the platform.

The Hoobrakes said good-bye and drove away quickly. Gloria waited near the bookstall while Mr. Lace collected the luggage. An old porter came up to the young salesman, touched his cap, and said, " Excuse me, sir, did a passenger leave a fur glove 'ere ? " The salesman spent two minutes banging piles of papers on the top of one another, and when the porter repeated his question, answered, " No 'e didn't," in a Cockney voice. The porter touched his cap and walked away. The roof leaked, and a succession of drops splashed the ground two feet from where Gloria was standing. No one seemed to be meeting any of the passengers who had come by the train.

Then Mr. Lace came up. They made a distribution of the luggage, and Gloria and Mrs. Lloyd-Muce got into one taxi, and Mr. Lace into another.

" I may be," he shouted, " a bit late. I've got to call somewhere on the way." And when he saw they were out of earshot, he gave his driver the address of a doctor in Wimpole Street; for he was still troubled by the fear (amongst others) that the ship's doctor might have been mistaken when he said that Mr. Lloyd-Muce's disease could not have been communicated to his wife, and could not, through her, be communicated to any future husband. On this and other points he was soon to be happily reassured.

Neither Gloria nor Mrs. Lloyd-Muce spoke during their drive. The rain leaked through the shut window of the taxi and a crack in the hood. Gloria was reminded of an afternoon, years before, when she had driven to school near Sevenoaks, alone in a four-wheeler. She felt that the memory was more real than the woman beside whom she was sitting or the street which they were passing.

Owing to some road repairs in Brompton Road, they drove into Lithe Street from the north end and passed No. 38, where Mr. Balcony had lived. The two yew trees in tubs, which had stood beside the door, had been taken away.

Blinds were drawn in all the windows, and the signs of three house-agents were fastened to the area railings.

At the *Maison Swing*, Mr. Lace's sister met them on the doorstep, and only ceased to smile when she mentioned that the business had made no profit, "while Hilary was away." Gloria had happened to notice the gloomy show in the shop window, but was unmoved. She said nothing, and, as soon as she could, went to her room. It was so stuffy that she had to open the window, in spite of the rain which was blown on to her dressing-table.

She did not trouble to unpack, but took off her hat, coat and shoes, and lay down on the bed. At first she hoped that she might be going to fall asleep and have a pleasant dream. But she could not, and, like one with frost-bitten fingers trying to untie a knot in a piece of thin string, she began to think of the future and to decide where, since she must go away, she would go, and what she would do. Each time, however, that her thoughts arrived at any clear idea, the associations of the past drove away all motives, hopes and plans, and in the end, when she had soothed herself for a short while with a memory more powerful than most, she was invaded by so intense and sudden a feeling of despair, that her whole body seemed to crumple up as if in a spasm of physical agony. " I can't bear it," she said to herself, " I can't bear it, any more. I shall scream and scream till they all come up and send me away." And she moaned aloud once or twice, but, thinking she heard a footstep on the stairs, continued her meditation in silence, while the light faded in the street and the dirty white mat on the dressing-table was drenched with rain.

. . . . .

Her son was born in due season, but her acquaintances, though they supposed him born out of wedlock, showed little surprise or disapproval. For the most part they were theatrical and artistic people, and she knew them, not so much because she liked them, as because other folk were more difficult to know.

THE END